# Bringing Back the Tree of Snow

# Bringing Back the
# Tree of Snow

R. E. Hammer

ISBN-13: 9780692997499
ISBN-10: 0692997490
Library of Congress Control Number: 2018901885

Typeset by Amnet Systems.

*For My Father*

# Part One: The Field Trip

# Chapter 1

Waking up and confronting a day with all its routine normalcy was often difficult for Noah Bradbury, especially if the alarm clock interrupted him right in the middle of a compelling dream. But today, December 2, 2084, waking up was easy. The entire seventh grade class at his school was going on a field trip to New York City, to visit the American Museum of Natural History. Looking out his bedroom window, Noah saw that the sun, as if wanting to partake of the day's adventure, was trying to break through the smudgy cloud system that usually hung overhead.

Throughout the fall, everyone in the seventh grade had been reading about Earth, its history and many environments. At the museum, they were going to see a movie—made from film footage taken from space shuttles over the past 100 years— about the small blue and white planet. Like almost everyone else in his school whose parents worked at the institute, Noah had been to the museum at least a hundred times. Still, he was looking forward to seeing the film and to hanging out in the museum with his classmates.

Looking about his small bedroom that was once again a cluttered mess, Noah wondered how he would find everything he needed for the day. Just last Thursday, the same room had been a perfectly clean one in which extra seating had been set up for Thanksgiving dinner guests. His parents had been hosting Thanksgiving dinner, for his grandparents and a few friends and neighbors, ever since he was a little kid. Their apartment at the research institute where both his parents worked was small, but with the use of his and his younger sister Madeleine's bedrooms, there was enough space for everyone. It was a day he looked forward to every year.

"Are you almost ready, Noah? You don't want to be late," his mother called to him from the family room.

"I'll be out in a few minutes," he yelled back.

As he washed with the new lavender-scented, bug-repelling sanitizer the institute had distributed to all its residents, he thought about the hot shower he would soon be able to take. His mother had promised both him and his sister that they could each have their own bath or shower to prepare for the upcoming holidays. Such luxuries were only permitted on special occasions. When he was younger, he had always chosen the bath option. After submerging his entire body in the warm water, he'd resurface, lie back, and daydream until his skin wrinkled and the water cooled. Now that he was thirteen and a teenager, it seemed more appropriate to take a shower as his father always did.

Digging through a mound of clean laundry, Noah retrieved the outfit he wanted to wear—jeans and his favorite T-shirt, the turquoise one with a graphic image of a whale on its front. After finding his red backpack, he gathered up the things he needed to put into it: his computer tablet and its charger, his money and identification cards, an oxygen mask, and a water bottle. Since it would most likely rain in the afternoon, he packed a rain poncho that rolled up into a tiny pouch.

Before leaving his room, he stopped to debate with himself about whether he should bring the book he was in the middle of reading. It was a great book, and whenever he picked it up he had a hard time putting it down. His mother would have to remind him repeatedly that he had homework or chores to do, or that it was time to go to sleep. Even though there would probably be no time to open it, he stuffed it into his backpack along with everything else.

Like his mother, Noah was a huge fan of science fiction and real, physical books. Reading was done mainly on a computer, but luckily his mother had inherited a collection of old hardcovers and paperbacks from her parents and grandparents which she shared with Noah. Their front and back covers held a large number of rustling pages between them, and even if Noah wasn't thrilled with a story, the process of reading one was itself rewarding. He enjoyed turning over each yellowing page and watching the stack of those he'd read grow thicker.

Out of all the books his mother had given him, the one he treasured most was one that had belonged to one of his great-great-grandmothers. On the inside cover of *A Wrinkle in Time*, she had written her name, Lillian, in ink, in a cursive handwriting when she was about the same age Noah was now. Even though he'd read the book many times and was now reading other great books, it was still his favorite.

When Noah was sure he had what he needed, he walked into the family room and dropped his backpack on the floor by the apartment's front door.

"That was more than a few minutes," Joanne Bradbury said, without looking up from her work.

"I know!" Noah shrugged, before walking into the tiny kitchen to pour himself a bowl of cereal.

Though the apartment Noah's family lived in was small, it had a warm and lovely atmosphere. The family room was filled with artwork. A colorful quilt made by one of Noah's grandmothers was displayed on a rack by the wall, and a real wool afghan that had been knit by one of his great-grandmothers was draped over the couch. Both were just for show, as it was never cold enough to need either of them.

Hanging on the walls were two paintings done by Lillian's husband, Sam, Noah's great-great-grandfather who had been a well-respected artist. One painting depicted a romantic scene of a couple walking on a road lined with flowering trees. The other was of a small purple and turquoise ocean wave, washing in and around yellow and red rocks. Noah would have happily jumped into either one of them. There was also a family portrait, done in a sort of abstract style, by Madeleine, an emerging artist as his father put it.

When Noah returned to the family room with his cereal, he sat down at the rectangular oak table where his mother was editing her doctoral dissertation. Long ago, the table had belonged to Sam, who had worked on his paintings and illustrations there. Now it was where his family gathered to eat meals, do homework, play chess, and assemble puzzles. Though many people frowned upon keeping such wooden furniture, given what was happening to the region's hardwood trees, Noah's mother refused to part with it. To her, the table was more than just a family heirloom, it was a family member.

Noah watched his mother as she sipped a mug of tea and scribbled notes on her paper. She was to present her dissertation to a committee just after the new year, and Noah admired how hard she'd been working on it. While finishing her doctorate in entomology, she also worked part-time in a laboratory with a team of scientists who were trying to propagate species of beneficial insects, those that pollinated plants and others that ate disease-carrying bugs. Joanne Bradbury worked with honey bees, butterflies, and even centipedes. One time a centipede she brought home escaped. After conducting a massive search for it, they found it under Madeleine's bed pulling dust bunnies out from its many legs.

"Thank goodness you're okay," his mother said to the bug while Maddie screamed her head off. It had been pretty hilarious.

While Noah finished eating his cereal, the cat arrived and wrapped himself around Noah's legs.

"Madeleine, come feed the cat!" his mother now hollered for his sister.

Noah had wanted a dog when he was younger, but there was little room in the apartment, so he had settled for visits to the institute's canine house. There, he had befriended a young female shepherd who was being trained as a security dog. From behind her enclosure, the shepherd would bare her teeth and growl, but once released she would wag her tail, jump up, and lick Noah's face with unrestrained happiness. One day for some unknown reason, she bit Noah's arm, and even though a healing gel was applied to the wound, the bite left a scar. Afterwards, Noah wanted nothing further to do with her or the canine house and resigned himself to being a cat owner.

Showing no sense of loyalty, the cat immediately ran away from Noah's legs when Madeleine, an annoying fourth grader who was still in her pajamas, arrived with his food. After putting the cat food on the floor, Madeleine sat down across from their mother and started talking nonstop about something a friend had done. Their mother looked up and made half-alert comments such as "Oh, how funny," and "I agree." No one would have guessed that Madeleine was recovering from an intestinal virus and had been sleeping for the past several days. Even though she sounded just fine to Noah, she would get to stay home from school again. But then Noah remembered that he too was getting out of having to sit in a classroom all day.

Though he sometimes complained about it, Noah did like the institute's school and knew he was lucky to be a student there. There were institutes all over the country, but the one where his family lived was one of the larger and more prestigious ones. They lived there because of the work his parents were doing. Often, he worried that something unexpected might happen and that his family, including his mother's parents who lived there as well, would have to move to a neighborhood like the one where his friend Joshua Peterson lived.

At first, only kids living at the institute could attend its school. But then, institutes everywhere were pressured into allowing nonresidents access to their facilities. Joshua, who had been a quiet and hard-working student in his school, was one of the kids selected for the commuter program. Now that Joshua was one of his closest friends, Noah had learned from him what life could be like elsewhere.

The institute was like an oasis surrounded by all kinds of turbulence. It resembled a university campus and had everything in it a small town would. Conservatories that housed trees, plants, insects, birds, and other small and domesticated animals, native to the Northeast occupied much of its grounds. Noah wished that larger animals such as bears and coyotes could also be housed there, but they were cared for in sanctuaries that had once been zoos or were located in state parks. Noah liked to visit the one in the Catskill Mountains where his father's parents lived.

"Hey, sport," Noah felt his father slap his back as he washed his breakfast bowl with sanitizing spray.

Noah was relieved to see his father in a better mood. All fall, Matthew Bradbury, had been struggling with his research team to find a cure for a terrible disease that was destroying Northeastern trees, especially the majestic hardwoods. The team of scientists suspected that the disease had been released from melting permafrost and had migrated in through warm ocean water. The cure they thought they'd found for it had just proved to be ineffective.

In the mornings, while they walked together to school and work, Noah saw how worried his father was. The Thanksgiving holiday had distracted him somewhat, but now that it had passed, Noah was afraid his dad would once again sink into despair.

"Good morning, Matthew," said his mother, getting up from her writing to kiss her husband's cheek.

"Noah, did you check to make sure you aren't forgetting anything?" she then asked him.

"I think I have everything, Mom."

"What about bug repellent? Did you remember that?" his mother the entomologist asked.

He had forgotten to pack bug repellent. Though Noah was responsible, he could be a bit spacey and often "had his head in the clouds" as his father would say. Noah's mother handed him a small container of bug repellent cream and a bag containing his lunch: a beef-flavored protein wrap, a bag of potato chips, an apple, and a berry-flavored vitamin drink. He crammed his lunch and the bug repellent into his backpack.

Every week Noah's father brought home a small bag of fruit and vegetables from the conservatories. In Noah's opinion, this was the best part of living at the institute. This Thanksgiving, he brought home apples, chestnuts, cranberries, potatoes, and squash. The turkey breast they had for dinner was the only thing that was not real. It was made from a protein substitute, though his grandfather, who had once eaten real turkey meat, said it looked and tasted like it was real.

When Noah stepped outside, he could feel the day would again be warm and humid. The year before, he'd gotten a sense of what the holiday season had once been like when he and his father had visited a tree sanctuary that was trying to simulate the long-ago winters of New York. During the winter months, the sanctuary lowered its temperature to thirty-two degrees Fahrenheit and kept the grounds inside covered with a thin layer of snow. Noah and his father had stood in that sanctuary, wearing no more than light windbreakers, shivering while white flakes fell around them.

As he walked with his father on the path that would bring him first to school and then his father to the lab where he worked,

Noah tried to imagine the institute's landscape covered in snow. The tropical trees now growing all over the grounds would probably not be very happy with such a scenario, but the young birch saplings they were approaching most likely would be. He and his father stopped to examine the white-barked trees that had been planted outdoors back in September. Kneeling on the ground, his father looked at the trunk and leaves of one of them.

"How is it, Dad?" Noah asked.

"It could be better," his father sighed.

Noah was grateful for the tropical trees that had been planted at the institute, even though his father disapproved of them. Matthew Bradbury viewed them as interlopers and aggressive competitors and believed that some of them were further harming the native trees by making the soil toxic for them. Not all scientists believed this was happening, though, and because many of the tropical trees offered shade and helped lower temperatures, they continued to be planted. Noah was just happy that the institute had allowed some of them to be decorated for the holidays. Everywhere, the fronds of palm trees were adorned with lights and student-made ornaments.

"Have a wonderful time today and don't forget to say hello to the whale," his father said when they arrived at Noah's school.

"Hey, why don't I walk with you to the lab," Noah offered. For some reason, he was not ready to separate from his father just yet.

"You don't want them to leave for the museum without you, do you?"

"No!" Noah had forgotten for a moment how happy he was to be going on this field trip. "Dad, please tell Mom thanks for the apple."

"You can tell her tonight when you get home."

"Okay," Noah smiled.

As his father walked away, Noah felt an urge to run after him. Instead, he watched him walk toward the greenhouses whose glass domes sparkled in the hazy sunlight. Noah then looked up at his school. Like the greenhouses, it was glassy and dome-shaped and reflected the landscape around it. Shifting the weight of his backpack on his shoulders, Noah hesitated before following the crowd of kids through its open doors.

# Chapter 2

Three electric-powered buses were lined up behind the school. When Noah boarded the one to which he was assigned, he found that his seat had been taken by a girl named Tessa Dubois. Though Noah didn't know Tessa personally, he knew a little bit about her from Joshua who commuted to school with her. A few years back, Tessa's entire family had caught a virus that had spread throughout the region, and while she had survived, her parents and sister had not. When she began receiving medical treatment at the institute, she also started going to school there. Though Joshua had become her friend, most of the other kids at school thought she was strange and avoided her.

"Hi!" Noah greeted her softly.

Tessa didn't respond. Instead, she turned away and fixed her gaze out the window.

"I think you're in my seat," Noah observed. Her unfriendliness was really the only thing that prompted him to mention it.

"If you don't mind, I don't feel like talking," she replied curtly.

The seat wasn't worth arguing over, and so Noah quietly sat down in the one next to her. Truthfully, he preferred the aisle seat anyway. All around them students were laughing and chatting happily, and Noah wished he had been seated with someone else. As the bus started to move, Noah looked out the window, past Tessa, at the gritty neighborhood that surrounded the institute. The sunshine made it look a lot nicer than it usually did. Sunlight sparkled off the sides of buildings and the leaves of trees, making them shimmer like emeralds.

One hundred years ago, the area had been an affluent one filled with maple, elm, and sycamore trees. Each beautiful home had been surrounded by acres of green lawn. After the ocean had reclaimed many coastal areas, businesses and people like a rising tide flooded the area. The region quickly evolved into an urban one, though evidence of its past—a few large colonial houses with wrap- around porches—were still tucked between the new buildings. Now, they were mostly doctors' offices.

As history buffs, both Noah and his dad were grateful that many old buildings were being preserved. The modifications made to protect them from severe weather thankfully didn't alter their appearance much. They both thought that the newer buildings, boxy structures made of glass and metal, were boring. The latest construction was the worst. These buildings were being made from compressed cubes of recycled materials: aluminum, foam, and plastic, all recovered from coffee cups, soda bottles, and vegetable cans excavated from old landfills.

As Noah was looking out the window, Tessa pulled a sketch pad from her purse and began to draw an image from the passing scenery.

"Are you an artist?" Noah asked forgetting that she had told him to refrain from speaking to her.

"Not really," she replied.

"My sister wants to be an artist," Noah told her, as he leaned in to get a closer look. "Wow, that's really good!"

"It's just nothing," said Tessa letting out an annoyed sigh, before turning her entire body away from him, enveloping the sketch pad within her closed-off self.

Not even flattery would win her over, and Noah could not understand what Joshua had found to like about her. Still, there must be something. Joshua was a pretty good judge of character and the kind of kid who never let the opinions of others influence how he felt about someone. Noah admired that about him, and he had to believe that if Joshua liked this girl, there was probably more to her than everyone else was seeing.

As the bus made its way to New York City, Noah took out his book and read quietly. When he finished his chapter, he looked up and saw that Tessa had fallen asleep. It was hard to believe she was supposed to be in the eighth grade. She was so pale and small looking. The virus she had caught had been a terrible one, and everyone Noah knew had been terrified of catching it.

While Noah regarded her, Tessa's tortoiseshell glasses suddenly slipped down over her nose. When she opened her eyes to push them back up, Noah quickly shifted his gaze out the window. He decided that Tessa might fit in better if she dressed differently. Her clothes and glasses were so old-fashioned look-ing. At the very least, she should do away with the ratty pink-and-green kerchief she was wearing.

When Tessa fell back to sleep, Noah tried to put her out of his mind. He looked out the window at the city which could now be seen in the distance as a toy-like cluster of geometric shapes. It kept disappearing behind tall buildings and reap-pearing in the narrow gaps between them. After each of these intervals, it grew progressively larger until finally after one lengthy disappearance, it reappeared as if a curtain had been lifted, close-up and in full view, just before the bus slipped into the tunnel.

Only authorized vehicles were allowed into New York City. At the end of the tunnel, the three buses stopped at a security checkpoint, and while they waited for clearance to enter the city, Tessa continued to sleep. Her cloth bag had fallen to the floor, and the kerchief she wore had loosened, revealing patches of pink scalp beneath a thin layer of brown hair. Now under-standing why Tessa wore the head covering, Noah felt guilty for judging how it looked.

When they arrived at the museum, Noah gently tapped Tessa's shoulder to wake her. He picked her cloth handbag up off the floor. A letter T was embroidered on its front in vibrant pink and green colors. Tessa's initial appeared to be designed to look like a flowering spring tree. Without saying anything, Noah handed Tessa her bag. He then stepped into the aisle and joined the line of students waiting to get off the bus.

The student's line snaked up the museum's steps and through its front doors, before spreading itself out, amoeba-like, within the Theodore Roosevelt Rotunda. All giggling and whispering stopped, and a hush fell over the crowd when the strictest teacher, Mr. Gerard, called for everyone's attention.

"Excuse me!" roared Mr. Gerard. "We have two hours to explore the museum this morning. At twelve o'clock we will all meet downstairs in the school lunchroom to eat. Afterwards, we will go to the Hayden Planetarium to see the movie. You should all be taking notes on this film, as information from it will be included on next week's test. If anyone feels sick or believes they are lost, they are to head down to the student lunchrooms where two of our parent volunteers will be waiting. No one is to step foot outside the museum. Is that understood?"

A sea of heads bobbed up and down in agreement, while Noah scanned the crowd looking for Joshua and their friend Miguel. Teacher-led groups had begun to form as Noah walked through the crowd to the Christmas tree, where he and his friends had planned to meet. Apparently, Joshua and Miguel had forgotten about this because when Noah reached the tree, they were nowhere to be seen. He tried calling them both on his tablet, but neither answered.

Even though it was a fake, the museum's Christmas tree was, as always, beautiful. The synthetic replica of a hemlock was decorated with tiny white lights and origami animals. Noah had made many origami birds and boxes before, but never anything as elaborate as the animals on the tree before him. It was hard to believe that a detailed *T. rex* had been made by folding just a single flat piece of paper.

When the groups began to embark for different halls and his friends were still nowhere to be seen, Noah followed the one heading toward the Hall of Ocean Life. Not only was the hall his favorite, but it was that of his father and grandfather as well.

For Noah, this was mainly because of the female blue whale. He was a real fanatic about whales in general, to which his T-shirt attested. But his attachment to the female blue whale was in part due to something that happened when he was just five years old.

During one of his family's visits to the museum, he became lost. It had been his own fault. His parents had bumped into a pair of their colleagues, and while they were engaged in conversation, Noah became impatient and took it upon himself to go into the gift store in search of a toy. When he stepped out of the store, he couldn't find his parents anywhere. He had wandered, small and frightened, searching for them through crowds of strangers, until he arrived at the Milstein Hall of Ocean Life. There, he'd walked through the crowded hall to a group of benches beneath the great leviathan, sat down in the front row, and waited.

Sitting beneath the great whale, Noah had felt calm and protected. He was not at all surprised when his father found him there. His father, on the other hand, had been very shaken and had immediately picked Noah up and hugged him. As they walked hand in hand to meet his mother and toddler sister, Noah told his father that when he grew up, he wanted to become the kind of scientist who helped protect the oceans. His father had said that his plan sounded like a wonderful one.

"Noah!" Miguel shouted out to him when he entered the Hall of Ocean Life. He was with two girls from his class, whom Noah didn't know.

"I looked for you but couldn't find you," claimed Miguel.

"I was waiting by the tree, which is where we were supposed to meet," Noah reminded him.

"I'm sorry, I forgot."

Miguel and Noah stood behind the two girls who were admiring a diorama of jellyfish.

"Hannah just told me that Keira thinks you seem nice," whispered a conciliatory Miguel.

"If you think someone is nice then you should say hi," replied Noah, moodily.

"She might be shy," Miguel pointed out.

Noah didn't say anything. He was still annoyed by that girl Tessa's attitude on the bus.

"By the way, Joshua is around here somewhere. He is with that girl he likes, Ashley," said Miguel.

"Oh yeah?" replied Noah who was also annoyed with Joshua for forgetting their plan.

Miguel's parents were both science writers who lived in the same building as Noah's maternal grandparents. When they were younger, Miguel's extroverted personality had conflicted with Noah's shy and introverted one. But when they both became friends with Joshua, they became friends with each other and began to appreciate and learn from their differences.

The two boys followed the girls over to a diorama of sharks, where a group of their classmates had gathered.

"My grandmother told me that last spring, a tiger shark was seen off a beach in the town where she lives," said a girl who stood in the group's center.

"I doubt it. A tiger shark hasn't been seen along the Atlantic coastline in years," noted one of the boys.

Another boy snuck up behind the girl who had spoken and grabbed her shoulders.

"Get away from me!" The girl pretended to be angry as she pushed the boy away.

"It's just that you would make such good shark food," the boy teased.

"Leave me alone," the girl retorted before she and another girl sauntered away. They leaned into one another whispering before turning around and smiling at the boys.

"That girl, Daniela, is so full of herself," said Hannah. "She's a total fake."

"Maybe!" said Miguel. "But I have to agree she would make great shark food."

Hannah pushed Miguel away as Daniela had done. While the two continued to argue playfully, Noah and Keira walked away to look at other dioramas in the room. Noah quickly discovered that Miguel had been right, Keira was shy, and he felt the burden to make conversation was on him. He was very relieved when they found Mr. Gerard talking to a group of their classmates about the blue whale.

Noah and Keira joined the group and stood quietly as they listened to Mr. Gerard. The teacher explained how in some areas of the ocean, high levels of carbon dioxide made sea water so acidic that plankton, the animal at the base of a food chain, could no longer survive. As a result, neither krill, a small animal that feeds on plankton, nor blue whales, the enormous mammal that feeds on krill, can survive in those areas either.

Noah already knew this, though he didn't say anything. He did not want to appear to be some kind of know-it-all. He looked at his classmates, some of whom were whispering and nudging one another and wondered if they were even listening. Why didn't Mr. Gerard, king of the teachers, stop and berate them? It bothered Noah to think that the information Mr. Gerard had just relayed hadn't even registered with them.

When he was finished speaking, Mr. Gerard told the group that he was going to walk to other exhibits and that anyone who wanted to could join him. Hannah and Keira wanted to look at the diamonds in the Hall of Minerals, while Miguel wanted to visit North American Mammals. But Noah was not ready to leave. He told Miguel to go on ahead and that he would catch up to him.

After the group left, Noah walked over to the spot where he had waited for his father so long ago and looked up at the massive blue whale.

"Do you remember me? I wish there were a way I could help you," he whispered.

"I don't think he's going to give you an answer," quipped a young man standing behind him.

Noah turned to see a young couple who looked as though they were in college. The young woman had her arm slung around the shoulders of the young man who had spoken. She was laughing, not in a mocking way, but rather in the way adults or those who think they are adults, do at a cute but naive child.

"Yeah, I know that," said Noah. He turned and walked quickly away toward the Hall of North American Mammals.

# Chapter 3

"Hey, Noah, we're over here!" Miguel called out to him. "Miguel, you're supposed to speak with a quiet voice in the museum," Noah called back.

"What's wrong with you?" asked Miguel.

"Nothing!" answered Noah.

"Maybe he spoke loudly to get your attention, because you don't always pay attention," suggested a voice behind them.

Noah turned around to see Joshua.

"I don't pay attention? Why didn't you remember that we were supposed to meet at the tree? Where've you been anyway?" asked Noah.

"I told you, he was busy following Ashley around," teased Miguel.

"She was actually following me around, but now she's with her friends," explained Joshua.

"I just met one of your other girlfriends on the bus," Noah informed him as they began strolling through the Hall of North American Mammals.

"Which one?" asked Joshua who had stopped to look at the battling moose.

"Tessa, but she's not exactly friendly."

"You would like her if you got to know her," Joshua assured him.

"I think you're the only kid in school that she'll talk to," said Noah.

"Maybe!" Joshua shrugged. "Hey, let's go look at the wolves."

The three boys walked into the narrow side hall, to a diorama in which two wolves were running side by side across a snowy landscape.

"I bet I could outrun them," boasted Miguel, when they arrived.

"I'd like to see you try that," Joshua countered.

"I could now that I'm wearing these," assured Miguel, showing off his new running shoes.

"Those won't help you at all. For one thing, look at what the wolves are running over," noted Joshua.

"I'm sure these would get me across that," said Miguel, though he sounded doubtful.

"Well, you will never be able to find out, so why argue about it?" said Noah.

Back in September, the three boys had joined an after-school runner's club. Three times a week the club met at the indoor gymnasium and ran laps around the track. A friendly rivalry had sprung up between Joshua and Miguel. Noah was just happy to know he could run longer and faster than he ever had before.

"Noah might have a girlfriend," Miguel teased, changing the subject.

"I don't know how anyone could like that girl," quipped Noah.

"Everyone likes Keira," countered Miguel.

"Oh, I thought you meant someone else," Noah replied.

"Whoa! You mean there is someone else?" Miguel asked excitedly.

"No Miguel! There isn't anyone," Noah clarified with annoyance.

As his friends walked ahead, Noah remained peering moodily into the wolves' diorama. He was considering various ways of getting his seat assignment changed on the return bus trip home, when a sudden movement startled him. Quickly, he jumped back from the display case.

"Hey!" he called out to his friends.

"What is it?" asked Miguel. He and Joshua had both turned around as Noah ran up to them.

"One of those wolves, it's like he looked at me or something," he told them breathlessly.

"It might be due to the lighting in this area," offered Miguel.

"No, I remember how his head was positioned when we got to his display," said Noah, though he was not completely sure.

"It's just your imagination," Joshua assured him.

As the three boys continued walking, Noah decided that Joshua was right. It was just his over-active imagination playing games again. Still, he was relieved to find Ms. Rebecca, his and Joshua's homeroom teacher, standing with a group of girls at the end of the hall by the diorama of mountain lions.

"How many people have a pet cat at home?" he heard her ask as they walked up to the group.

He noticed that Tessa was among them, and that she was one of the few girls who did not raise her hand.

"Surprisingly, mountain lions are much like the common house cat," Ms. Rebecca continued.

"Do any of them still exist anymore?" asked Daniela, the girl whom Hannah had called a fake.

"Yes, there are many cougars still living. They live in different animal sanctuaries throughout the country. Like most large animals, they can no longer live independently," answered Ms. Rebecca.

"There are plenty of street cats everywhere. Why can't the mountain lion live on its own like they do?" Noah thought Daniela's interest, in cats at least, seemed genuine enough.

"Because the lives of street cats are more closely aligned with humans," replied Noah's pale, bespectacled seatmate.

"I had actually asked Ms. Rebecca," Daniela pointed out.

"Tessa is right. Animals whose lives are closely tied to our own have a greater chance of surviving in our world," explained Ms. Rebecca. Just then her tablet started to ring. She excused herself and stepped away to answer it.

"I wonder if mountain lions purred?" asked Daniela, sounding as if she were purring.

"They are called cougars, and of course they did," answered Tessa with a sneering tone in her voice.

"Wow, someone knows a lot about cats." Daniela's sarcasm elicited laughter from her friends.

Noah could understand why Daniela found Tessa's attitude annoying. Even if Tessa were as knowledgeable about cougars as he was about whales, it didn't mean she should show off.

"Too bad you can't scratch it behind its ears," said Miguel.

"No animal is an it. They are he or she," corrected Tessa.

At that, Daniela gave Tessa a look of mock horror and walked away with her friends.

Ms. Rebecca, who was still on her tablet's phone, seemed to be unaware of the social drama going on among the students. While the rest of the group moved on to look at other dioramas, Noah remained behind. He wanted to ask Ms. Rebecca if he could step outside for a bit. Suddenly, he felt very warm and even a little queasy.

While waiting, Noah's eye caught another movement, this time from within the cougar's diorama. Walking up to the display, he stared as the female mountain lion turned her head ever so slightly, looked directly at him and blinked her eyes.

"What's the matter?" asked Joshua, who had walked quickly over with Miguel when Noah cried out.

"That cougar just blinked its eyes at me," Noah told him.

"Remember, a cougar is not an it—therefore, *she* blinked her eyes at you. Maybe she likes you," joked Miguel.

"What's wrong, Noah?" asked Ms. Rebecca. She had finally finished her phone call.

"He thinks some of the animals are trying to interact with him," explained Miguel.

"It's not funny," said Joshua. "He might be hallucinating, and that's a symptom of all kinds of things."

"Joshua is right! Tessa, isn't it time for you to take your medicine?" Ms. Rebecca called out to her. "Why don't you walk with Noah to the cafeteria?"

Tessa looked up from the museum brochure she was studying.

"I'm fine!" Noah responded quickly.

Noah felt sure of what he saw. Still, hallucinations did often seem real.

"Noah, I am telling you to walk with Tessa to the cafeteria. I'll call to let the parent volunteers know you are on your way. You should eat something and maybe take some oxygen."

"It's for the best," whispered Miguel. "We're about to go upstairs to the dinosaur exhibit. If a wolf and mountain lion are giving you a hard time, I don't want to even think about what might happen there."

Noah ignored him. He now wondered if Ms. Rebecca thought he and Tessa would make a nice couple or something. First a shared seat assignment and now a stroll to the cafeteria.

"Fine!" said Noah, even more irritated than before. He walked alongside Tessa, only this time he refused to look at her. When they arrived at the staircase leading to the lower level, it was Tessa who broke the silence.

"I'm sorry for being nasty on the bus. I was angry at my foster mother. She told me there'd be too much walking on this trip, and she ordered me to stay home and clean the apartment instead. I came anyway."

"It's fine!" said Noah.

"She thinks I'm strong enough to do house cleaning but not to go on a field trip," vented Tessa. "I wish my doctor and the foster care agency would see what kind of a person she really is. I don't think they even care."

"I am sorry that your foster mother is so terrible," said Noah, who truthfully was.

"It doesn't matter," she replied.

"It does matter. You know, I really liked that drawing you were doing on the bus," Noah told her.

"Thanks! I'm just learning."

"My great-great-grandfather was a famous artist. We have his work hanging in our apartment."

"Could I see it sometime?"

"Oh, definitely!"

"Can I ask you a question?" Tessa asked.

"Sure," said Noah looking at her.

"It is true I sometimes talk to the stray cats in my neighborhood. But aside from that, do I give the impression that I'm weird or crazy?"

"I don't know! My sister sometimes talks to our cat, so maybe. But remember, you are asking someone who just thought he saw two stuffed animals come back to life."

"Well, it takes one to know one," Tessa smiled.

"Then, no! I don't think you are crazy," Noah smiled back at her.

"Then I promise you, I believe you and don't think you're crazy either," Tessa answered, looking at Noah intently.

Though she could have continued touring the museum after taking her medication, Tessa decided to remain in the cafeteria.

"You're missing the dinosaur exhibit," Noah told her.

"That's okay! I will see it another time," she replied.

For the rest of the morning, they sat together. Tessa worked on a drawing of the cougars, while Noah read his book. Now and then Noah looked up at her and felt a strange feeling. He remembered his father telling him that when he first met his mother he didn't like her.

At lunchtime, Joshua and Miguel joined them at their table. When Joshua looked at Noah and raised his eyebrows, Noah shrugged his shoulders, smiled shyly, and turned away. Neither he nor Tessa felt much like talking, and so they listened as mostly Miguel talked. After eating a few bites of his wrap, Noah gave his apple and chips to Joshua. He just wasn't hungry for them.

When lunch was over, Noah assured Ms. Rebecca that he felt fine. He joined his classmates as they walked once more through the first-floor halls on their way to the Planetarium. When they reached the crowded Hall of New York State though, Noah once again began to feel overheated. His T-shirt became so damp with sweat that the whale on its front looked like it really was immersed in water. Stopping to catch his breath, he joined a group of people who were gazing into a diorama.

Noah had seen and walked by *An October Afternoon Near Stissing Mountain* on numerous occasions. But as he stood looking at its mountainous landscape, covered by a sea of golden trees, he felt as though he were seeing it for the first time. His whole being filled with longing. How he wished he could step onto its trail and hike through all that nature, escaping for a bit from his overcrowded, overheated world.

The diorama had been painted a long time ago, and Noah tried to imagine what the real mountain must have been like. As he did, he began to feel a sensation of cool air rush toward him. The air seemed to be coming from some unseen vent, and Noah wondered if the people standing beside him felt it as well. Whether real or imagined, he was grateful for the cool air as it helped to revive him. He was about to resume his walk to the Planetarium, when a rough voice called his name.

"Noah, let's go!" barked Mr. Gerard who had walked all the way back to find him.

Ms. Rebecca must have taken attendance and reported him as missing. Noah followed the teacher into the Grand Gallery, where once again he had an urge to stop, this time in front of the Great Canoe. He read the plaque beneath it that described the canoe as having been made from a single cedar tree. Noah could not imagine how a tree could grow so large. Walking around the canoe, he admired the paintings of ravens and killer whales on the boat's bow and stern. He was wondering if the carved sea wolf beneath the bow was meant to be frightening, when he was startled once more by the sound of Mr. Gerard's voice.

"Noah, focus!" the teacher roared.

This time Mr. Gerard told Noah to walk in front of him as they made their way to the other side of the museum. When they arrived at the Planetarium's entrance, a guard brought them up in an elevator to the darkened theater where the seventh grade occupied practically every seat. The film, *Earth: A Planet Alone*, had just begun. Noah who preferred an aisle seat, something Miguel had told him was a sure sign of introversion, was not happy that the only seat he could find was in the middle of a row.

Squishing by several pairs of his classmates' knees, Noah glanced up at the huge ceiling screen. The theater had become a virtual space shuttle in which his class was traveling to the small planet that hovered overhead. As they approached the frosty blue-and-white Earth, it grew larger and larger in the surrounding sea of darkness until it filled the screen. Upon reaching his seat, Noah sat down and looked up at the moving and curving edge of the planet. When the shuttle dove into Earth's atmosphere, everyone's seat began to vibrate as if the theater were a real spacecraft being pulled in by Earth's gravity.

The multi-sensory experience held everyone's attention, which was why only those students whose knees Noah once again had to brush past, noticed when he left the theater. When the camera swirled down through the clouds, Noah had felt the theater swirl around as well, and when it plunged into the surface of the ocean, the feeling of dizziness overwhelmed him.

Sitting in the anteroom, just outside the theater, was a man who looked to be Noah's grandfather's age, dressed as an American Indian.

"May I help you?" the man asked Noah.

"I just need the restroom," Noah told the man who looked to be a museum attendant.

"These restrooms are being cleaned, but I can show you to another one," offered the attendant.

There was a yellow sign placed by the bathrooms that read Temporarily Closed.

"Okay, thank you," said Noah.

"Follow me," said the attendant who lead Noah out of the Planetarium.

"Hey, I hope the play is terrific. But try not to break any legs," laughed one of the two security guards who were standing just outside the Planetarium's entrance. The attendant, who apparently was also an actor, smiled and waved at the guards.

They walked to a bank of elevators, where the attendant inserted a plastic card into a reader mounted on the wall. When the elevator arrived, they stepped into it and rode up to an area of the museum not meant for the public. Noah had been to the offices of scientists, but this area was an unfamiliar one. Though he had begun to feel uneasy, Noah could find no reason to distrust the elderly actor. He continued to follow him along a corridor until they stopped at one of the closed doors. Using the same keycard he'd used to call the elevator, the man unlocked the restroom door.

"Thank you," Noah said feeling relieved. The man nodded and walked away.

Inside the restroom, Noah was surprised to find a sink with running water. Most bathrooms only offered hand sanitizing gels. He was quite thirsty, so he filled his cupped hands from the sink's faucet and drank numerous handfuls of the bland-tasting, yet sterilized, city water. He then sat down on the floor, leaned back against the wall, and closed his eyes.

After dozing briefly, Noah woke with a start. Quickly, he got up to return to the Planetarium; but as he did, the floor began to tilt back and forth, as if a huge wave moved beneath its surface. The sink, an overhead light, and a wastebasket all began to spin about the room as if caught in a cyclone. Noah fell to the floor and lost consciousness.

# Chapter 4

Like the planet Earth, Noah woke up to find himself alone and surrounded by darkness. In a state of disorientation, he frantically pawed at the ground, until his hand came to rest on the smooth nylon surface of his backpack. Reaching inside, he found his computer tablet and immediately turned it on. The sound of its comforting two-note bell broke the silence and as his trusted companion came to life, so did its much taken-for-granted light.

Now that Noah could see his surroundings, he remembered what had happened and where he was. He had no idea how long he'd been asleep. Immediately, he typed his parents' phone number into his computer.

"Come on, come on," he whispered while waiting for them to pick up.

For some reason, the call did not go through, and so he tried again and then again. When these attempts also failed, Noah restarted his computer and then, instead of calling his parents, he placed a call to the city's emergency number. But that call also failed, and Noah realized that something, he did not know what, was not working.

Earlier that day, the museum's Internet connection had been just fine. Everyone had been using their computer phones, even Ms. Rebecca who had answered a phone call just before... The events of the day came back to him: he had not been feeling well and was sent to the cafeteria to rest with Tessa. Later, after feeling dizzy during the film, he'd left the Planetarium, and a museum attendant had brought him to this bathroom. But before all that happened, a stuffed animal had blinked its eyes at him.

Noah filled with fear. What if he had been bitten by an insect? They carried all kinds of terrible diseases that caused hallucinations.

"That's not possible," he told himself.

Just that morning he'd used the new sanitizing wash that the institute was distributing. Supposedly, it was the most effective wash yet at keeping bugs away. Still, he should have applied the insect repellent that his mother had given him. He reached into his backpack and found its container. If he had been bitten by some bug, applying the cream now wouldn't help matters. The only thing he could try to do was get to a doctor.

The time on Noah's tablet read 1:15 pm, which was about the time he had left the theater. He had no idea what the present time was, but most likely it was much later than that. Hoisting his backpack onto his shoulders, Noah held the tablet in front of him and walked to the restroom door. He shook and shook the door handle, but it would not open. Didn't the person who locked the door see him lying there conked out on the floor?

"Hello! Is anyone there?" Noah called out, but no one answered.

Knowing that people often worked in the museum all night, Noah couldn't understand why Internet reception would be turned off. He sat down and this time tried sending a text message to his parents and the city's emergency number. While he was typing, he was interrupted by what sounded like the rustling of a skirt just outside the bathroom door.

"Ms. Rebecca, is that you?" Noah called softly through the door. He put the computer down, stood up, and waited. No one answered.

Again Noah turned the door handle. This time it opened easily, which meant someone must have just unlocked it. Stepping hesitantly into the quiet, dimly lit hall, Noah looked in both directions. He had expected to find whoever had rescued him waiting outside, but no one was there. There was no one to be seen anywhere.

Pins prickled along the back of Noah's neck as he walked quickly to the elevators. After pressing the call button, he waited anxiously, listening to the rattle and whirring hum of the approaching car. It seemed to take forever, and when it finally arrived, Noah felt a mixture of relief and trepidation as he stepped into its empty, windowless space. He pressed the button for the third floor and stood still while the metal box slowly descended. When the elevator released him, Noah walked to the Planetarium. It was now closed, and he realized that the entire museum was probably closed as well. Leaning against a wall, he looked around and tried to decide what to do.

When he was little, Noah used to wake his father up in the middle of the night when he had to use the bathroom. He was always sure some monster was lurking in the shadows of their minuscule apartment. Though his father continually tried to reassure him that there were no monsters, that it was just his imagination, Noah never bought it and continued to demand his father's company whenever he woke up at night.

Now at thirteen years old, as he stood alone considering the enormity of the museum before him and its maze of cavernous halls, he tried once more to reassure himself with his father's logic. It still brought him no comfort. The mystery of who had opened the door to the bathroom, and the possibility that he had not been hallucinating in the Hall of North American Mammals, both haunted him. Noah strained his ears listening for any wave of sound, a shut door, a footstep, a sigh, traveling in from the museum's furthest reaches. But the only sound was a low buzzing noise, emanating from a broken security light above a nearby exit sign.

Noah decided that the best thing to do was to head to the main entrance at the Theodore Roosevelt Rotunda, where his class had assembled earlier. It seemed to be where he would most likely find a security guard on duty. To get there, he would walk across the third-floor balcony in the Great Hall of African Mammals. He planned to keep his head down while doing so. No matter what, he would refrain from looking at any of the animals.

When he arrived at the Great Hall, he found that like the rest of the museum, it was lit only by nighttime security lights. Keeping his eyes focused on the floor, he walked across the balcony until he reached the middle of the room. There, he stopped and broke the promise he'd made to himself and looked up and around at the enormous gallery.

The hall was still. There was no sound whatsoever, not even the gentle whirring of an electric generator or air ventilator. Noah had never heard absolute silence before. What made it so frightening was an accompanying feeling that something knowing and seeing was present, whose silence was a way of communicating, who at any time might reveal itself in a dramatic and unannounced way.

There was no movement coming from any of the animals in this hall. They remained lifeless, mere mannequins posed for posterity in painted replicas of their natural habitats. Noah walked by the white rhinoceros, impala, and mandrill, stopping by the chimpanzees where he brazenly stared at them, daring them to respond. If any mischief were to happen in this hall, most likely they would be involved. But they refused to comply.

When he reached the end of the Great Hall, he looked down at the herd of elephants.

"Why won't you look at me?" he challenged them recklessly.

His adrenaline rose as he stared at them, willing that just one would raise his trunk and cry out the way he'd heard them do in old movies. But none did, and a new emotion took the place of his fear—one of sadness. The silence did communicate something after all. It spoke of absent voices, the missing ruckus and rumble of the hall's many animals.

At the museum's main entrance, there were no security guards or scientists to be found anywhere, only the dinosaurs, menacing Allosaurus and Barosaurus who stood like a sentinel protecting her young. Thankfully, the lights on the Christmas tree had been left on, and Noah sat down by its side, plugged his computer into an outlet, and leaned back against the wall.

Looking up at the fake hemlock, Noah recalled his father telling him how the tradition of tree lighting began with an ancient people who set trees on fire to bring light during the darkest time of the year. Though the hemlock lacked the piney smell that real ones had, it was still lovely, and it brought him comfort. He looked up at the many origami animals whose iridescent papers glittered among the tiny white lights. Peeking out from the tree's green branches were an orange-and-black striped tiger, a yellow dotted butterfly, a purple triceratops, and a blue speckled whale. Though he knew it was wrong to do so, Noah stood up, reached into the tree, and slipped the whale off its branch.

After putting the whale in his pocket, Noah walked to the museum's front doors and tried to push them open. As he'd expected, they were locked shut. Through their glass, he looked out at the park beyond. There, moths and other winged insects fluttered in the lights cast by antique street lamps. On such a warm December night, there were sure to be all kinds of unpleasant creatures roaming the streets: huge rats, feral cats, and even people who slipped in and out of the shadows, searching for ways to be entertained. It was probably safer to remain locked in the museum.

Returning to his spot by the tree, Noah again leaned back against the wall and closed his eyes while waiting for his tablet to charge. His mind began to meander, and as it drifted toward sleep, it led him along a path through the museum, back to the institute, and home to his apartment. Suddenly, a sense of alarm woke him and brought him back to the museum. Sitting up, he remained still as his eyes moved over the perimeter of the Theodore Roosevelt Rotunda.

At the far end of the room were shadows that appeared to be moving. One was changing its size and shape as a cloud does when moving across the sky. What looked like a crooked nose on a man's face, grew and lengthened into the form of a dog. Grabbing his backpack, Noah got up and walked quickly to the nearest staircase. Jumping down the stairs two at a time, he landed on the first floor with a thud before running all the way to the Hall of Ocean Life. He knew that here, just like he'd been so long ago as a lost and frightened child, he would be safe.

He walked to the hall's second level where less than twenty-four hours ago his classmates had gathered. How he wished they were here with him now. Sitting down next to the great white shark, he contemplated the irony of seeking security from what had been one of the world's most dangerous creatures. Without the presence of an actual ocean though, he felt sure that not even a hallucination could bring the fearsome fish back to life.

While listening to the sound of his heart, or an artery beating in his ears, Noah tried to calm himself. He reflected on the nature of shadows, how even at home in his small room their shapes shifted in the changing light. The moving shadow most likely had a rational explanation. But it was what had happened in the restroom that was still worrying him. Someone had unlocked the door and though that person had not wanted to be seen, whoever it was knew of his lonely presence in the museum. Noah wrapped his arms around his knees. Morning could not arrive soon enough.

Since it was possible that the Hall of Oceans had the Internet service that other areas of the museum lacked, Noah reached into his backpack for his computer. At the very least, he wanted to find out what time it was. But his computer was missing, and after a few moments of confusion, he realized what he'd done. In his state of panic, he'd left his computer charging by the Christmas tree. Noah utterly depended on his computer and he had no choice but to leave the security of the great whale's domain and return to the shadows by the main entrance to retrieve it.

Distracted by the anger he felt at himself, Noah left the Hall of Ocean Life and walked with his head down into the Hall of Biodiversity, without even noticing the large canine who looked out at him from the African rainforest. He was walking into Memorial Hall, toward a staircase that would bring him to the second floor, when a low and mournful howl sounded behind him. Slowly, he turned around. There, standing several yards away, was a wolf.

"Even if you're terrified, don't let it show. Just casually walk away," Joshua had once advised him on how to deal with bullies. "They are less likely to go after someone who is not afraid of them. Your fear is your worst enemy, and if you let it, it will make a mess of everything."

Trying to ignore the wolf, as if the animal were just another hallucination, Noah turned away and walked quickly to the staircase. When he reached its top, he looked back once more. Unlike Miguel, he knew with certainty that regardless of the kind of sneakers he wore, he would never be able to outrun a wolf. For the time being, the animal remained still. Only his eyes, yellow and narrow like two half-moons, followed Noah.

"Just breathe," Noah told himself, as he headed to the main entrance, trying to maintain his normal walking gait.

From somewhere behind him, the wolf howled once more and Noah, forgetting all about retrieving his computer, began to run to the other end of the museum. When he arrived at the Rose Space Center, he ducked under a barrier and ran to the glass doors that led to the park. This exit too was now locked. After banging on the glass with his fists, Noah flailed his arms about like a maniac hoping someone would be out there to see him. He thought he saw a nighttime prowler waving back at him, but it was only the swaying limbs of a young tree.

Another howl let Noah know that the wolf was following him. In search of refuge, he ran up the Scaling Walkway that spiraled up to the planetarium's sphere. However, it too was now closed. Upon realizing that the wolf could easily trap him there, Noah quickly ran back down. Like a small animal desperately trying to avoid becoming prey, Noah jumped down the escalator that led to the first floor, two steps at a time.

Arriving in the Hall of the Universe, he looked up at a new work of art that had recently been installed there. It was a stone sculpture of a featureless man and woman reaching their arms up like zombies toward the celestial bodies hanging over their heads. Noah regarded it scornfully, wondering why anyone would make such a thing, when it suddenly helped him realize something. He was the son of two scientists, members of what was arguably the bravest group of people anywhere. Rather than run away from what was unknown and frightening, they sought it out and strived to understand it.

Here he was, in one of the most important science museums in the world: a place where the past and present collide, where his computer was now overcharging just a few feet away from dinosaur skeletons. This museum held invaluable resources and treasures that helped scientists like his parents solve mysteries and make discoveries. While running through its halls, Noah had been so afraid that the museum's purpose had been the furthest thing from his mind. Now though, he realized what he must do. Gathering up all his strength, he bravely headed back to the Hall of North American Mammals.

The hall, now cast in a reddish glow, appeared as benign as the Hall of African Mammals had. But when Noah walked to the center of the first gallery, he realized this was not so. He tried to remain calm and keep his feet rooted to the floor, as he watched the enormous brown bear lift his muzzle and sniff the glass-enclosed air. Though their movements were subtle—a tossing of a head, a shift in weight from one foot to another—in every diorama in the hall the mammals of North America began to come back to life.

Quickly, Noah darted into the side hallway where the smaller animals rustled in their display cases. When he reached the wolves' diorama, he found that, as he'd expected, only one of them remained. How Noah wished his new cat-loving friend were here to help him figure out what was happening. Bravely, he hurried on to the diorama of her favorite animal.

Walking up to the cougar's diorama, Noah watched as the female cat began to pace restlessly back and forth while her mate, lying nearby, licked his paws and ignored them both. Were it not for the glass that separated them, Noah could have easily reached out and touched their wheat-colored fur. Noah was observing them when, without any warning, the female cat cried out. From somewhere just outside the rear exit, the wolf howled in response.

The sound of it served as a starting signal. With Joshua's advice now forgotten, Noah's fear took over and he began to run. Past the bears, bison, and moose; past the diorama of New Amsterdam in Memorial Hall; through the Halls of Biodiversity and Forests; the act of running itself only worsening Noah's fear.

At the end of the Hall of New York State, Noah stopped at the diorama where he had stood earlier that day—or was it now the day before? As he gasped for breath, his legs buckled beneath him and just before he again lost consciousness, a thought occurred to him: *They have the wrong Noah.*

# Chapter 5

Once again, Noah was revived by air blowing in from somewhere near the diorama of *Stissing Mountain*. It was chillier than it had been before, and Noah took his rain poncho out of its sack and slipped it over his head. It was not nearly warm enough. Folding his legs into his chest, he wrapped his arms around them and shivered.

As Noah gazed groggily at the autumn scene, the little red fox walked up to the glass, sniffed the air, and looked out at him. The red-leafed bushes rustled in the cool breeze, and the noisy sounds of geese and ducks rose from the lake below. Just as two blue jays took off in flight, Noah spotted a black crow flying toward him from the mountains. When the crow swooped into the museum, Noah realized that the glass encasing the diorama had disappeared.

The bird landed on the nearby exit sign and was studying Noah with a coal black eye, when the wolf reappeared from around a bend in the hall. Unable to move, Noah was looking from one to the other when suddenly the bird let out a loud caw and flew back toward the mountains. The nimble wolf snatched Noah's backpack off the floor and then followed the bird into the diorama. Standing on the dirt path, the wolf looked out at Noah. It was as if the canine were playing a game, waiting for Noah to now chase him. After several minutes the wolf, still carrying the backpack in his teeth, trotted along the trail until he was out of view.

Without stopping to consider that the contents of his backpack—identification cards, a water bottle, and bug repellent—were just things that could have easily been replaced, Noah followed the wolf into the diorama hoping to retrieve them. The wolf was standing on the trail a short distance away. Noah's attention though, was quickly diverted, and he forgot all about his backpack and the wolf, as he looked around in disbelief.

The panoramic view encompassed a distance as far and wide as any in a real world. Noah looked out over the lake and mountains to the endless sky and landscape beyond. Perhaps he was viewing a three-dimensional film projection in a theater like the one at the Planetarium. In the same way that the film *Earth: A Planet Alone* had allowed his class to experience outer space, maybe this film was intended to provide visitors with an experience of the natural world as it once had been.

Noah's senses contradicted this theory though, as each one registered the realness of the space around him. He could feel the hard ground beneath his sneakers, and the wind of a long-ago autumn brushing past his face. He could hear the voices of birds and smell the earthy scents of damp wood, water, herbs, and burnt leaves that filled the air.

When Noah turned to look for the entrance he'd just stepped through, he found an alcove embedded in a rocky cliff.

He walked over to the alcove and peered through its jagged edge. He could still see the museum clearly, its shiny polished floor and the exit sign at the end of the hall. At the sound of someone calling his name, he turned around.

"Welcome to our world, Noah," greeted a man who had appeared on the trail below.

It was an immense relief to finally be in the presence of another human being. Though much younger than the man who had brought Noah up on the elevator to the restroom, this man too was dressed as an American Indian. Perhaps they were both a part of the same theatrical group, one that performed historical plays.

"Where are we? Is this a theater or another one of the museum's halls?" Noah asked him.

"This is not a theater or a hall. This world is my home," said the man. "My name is Taman. You have stepped from your world back in time to mine. Are you hungry?"

Without waiting for an answer, the man walked over to a leather bag that was leaning against a rock. He unpacked a flatbread and what looked to be pieces of protein meat. Noah hadn't eaten much of anything during the past twenty-four hours. Putting all other concerns aside, he sat on the ground, wrapped the protein strips in the bread, and began devouring the food. The protein strip was saltier, more flavorful and its texture grainier, than anything Noah had ever eaten before.

"What kind of meat is this supposed to taste like?" Noah asked.

"It's smoked deer meat," answered Taman.

Noah put the wrap down and looked up at him.

"Finish eating. It is good for you," said Taman.

Noah was so hungry that he continued eating without questioning it further. When he next looked up, he saw that the wolf, whom he had forgotten all about, was still carrying his backpack. Noah stood up and backed away.

"He will not hurt you, Noah. He is a friend. It was his job to guide you into our world," assured Taman.

"How do you know who I am?" asked Noah.

"The animals have observed you over the years. They no longer live in your world, but their spirits may return from the past and appear in their old forms. They can be seen only by those they choose."

After dropping Noah's backpack by Taman's feet, the wolf remained. Though he was much larger than the female shepherd who lived at the institute, Noah thought he resembled that unpredictable canine who had bitten him.

"We must not detain him any longer. He has his own family to attend to," said Taman, handing Noah his backpack. The wolf then walked down the trail and disappeared into the trees.

"How is it possible that I've traveled back in time?" Noah asked.

"The museum is a gateway to the past," said Taman.

Noah looked at the lake and the mountains and what seemed to be an infinite number of trees. It most certainly did not look like his world.

"Why didn't my friends see the animals come to life?"

"Only you expressed a wish to help them," Taman smiled.

"Did I?" Noah then remembered how he had addressed the whale in the Hall of Oceans.

"Your world, the world of our children, is in trouble. Our native trees are dying, and soon those of other lands will follow."

Noah recalled the look on his father's face while he examined the young birch tree at the institute.

"Yes, I know that," said Noah. "My father is a scientist who is working hard to find a way to save them. I can introduce you to him and to the other scientists he works with."

But Taman shook his head and put his hand up, asking Noah to wait and hear him.

"It is told that an ancient white oak is still alive in our world. She is a tree of legend, believed to have an ability to heal other trees. She will not exist for much longer. You are being asked to find her and bring one of her acorns back to your world."

"Many scientists who work in the museum know all about trees. I think it would be better to ask one of them to help you find this tree. I'm only thirteen years old."

"The Great Oak will be found only by one she chooses. The animals believe she will choose you," said Taman.

Noah regarded Taman, who appeared to be about the same age as Noah's father. With a handsome face and dark eyes that expressed warmth and intelligence, Taman just didn't seem like the kind of person who would be trying to deceive him.

"All creatures depend on the survival of Earth's trees," said Taman softly, referring to the paper whale Noah had taken out of his pocket. "Without trees, there would be no oxygen. If an offspring of the white oak is planted in your world, the trees, and many animals as well, will have a greater chance of surviving."

Looking down, Noah kicked the rocks by his feet. As he turned the origami whale over in his hands, he recalled a story his father had once told him. It was a story about three teenagers who had influenced the movement to build greenhouses specifically designed to preserve the genetic material taken from fallen trees.

Long ago, even before his grandfather had been born, a hurricane had swept through New York, uprooting many of the region's majestic, old giants. After the storm, the three ninth graders began collecting cuttings and seeds from the fallen trees in their town, some of which were well over one hundred years old. They brought these cuttings and seeds back to their school, where they rooted and planted them. School officials were so pleased with the students' efforts that they decided to build a greenhouse for the new saplings. When the greenhouse was completed, the students dubbed it *The Sanctuary for Lost Trees.* Soon schools all over the country began to build greenhouses of their own to protect the trees in their communities.

After Noah heard this story of the three teenagers, he vowed that he too would do something monumental when he reached their age. Now that he was thirteen, he could think of nothing more important than being able to help his father with his mission to save the Northeast's hardwood trees.

"Okay!" Noah said looking up at Taman. "If you really believe this oak tree will save the trees in my world, then I will try to help you find it. But I need to see a doctor first. I may have been bitten by a bug and contracted a virus."

"You have been preparing to enter our world. Now that you are here, you should no longer be troubled by dizziness."

"Yes, but I still need to let my family know where I am. And would it be possible to ask a friend to help me?

"Whoever seeks the Great Oak must do so alone," said Taman. "There is no time to speak with your family. The path between our worlds will soon close."

Noah looked out at the mountains and sky.

"What do I have to do?" Noah asked, shifting his gaze back to Taman.

"The first thing you must do is leave all your belongings in the museum. Material things may only travel from the past into the future with the movement of time."

Taman gave Noah an armful of clothing. Stepping through the alcove and into the museum, Noah quickly changed into the soft leather pants, tunic, and moccasins. He then folded up his clothes and neatly placed them, along with his sneakers and backpack, on the museum's floor. Noah peered at the red exit sign. It was not too late to change his mind. Instead, he placed the origami whale he had taken from the Christmas tree on top of his backpack and stepped back into the diorama.

He did so just in time. A ray of light from the sun setting over the mountains hit the alcove. In a fiery glare, the sun reflected off the glass that had spread across the alcove and encased the diorama back in the museum. Noah looked at the alcove and watched as the glass crackled like frosted ice and turned into what looked like a crystallized quartz. Soon all visibility from the world of the past into the museum was obstructed. When the sun's rays moved away, the quartz disappeared, and the small alcove was filled in with granite rock.

"You have arrived in our world during autumn as depicted in the diorama," Taman said. "Though you will be in this world for two and a half months, you will be away from your world for only one month. You must leave our world by midnight on the day before the arrival of the winter solstice. You will return to your own just after midnight at the start of your new year."

Taman pointed north. "My home is in the valley just beyond those woods. We should arrive there in an hour's time."

There was not a road to be seen anywhere. There were no buildings, brightly lit billboards, or humming drones flying overhead. Only the voices of birds were heard, who Taman said talked to one another and increased their chatter at sunset. What mostly existed were trees, multitudes of them, marching off in every direction.

The western edge of the sky was now streaked with pinks and reds that mingled with the deepening blue. Noah walked behind Taman, following his footsteps as best he could, as they made their way along the trail to the forest below. Tired from running through the museum all night, Noah struggled to walk in the unfamiliar moccasins which felt so different from his thick heeled running shoes. Each rock and tree root he carelessly stepped on registered through the moccasins' soles.

When they stepped into the forest, the world became dark. Taman motioned for Noah to walk in front as they made their way over the now moss-covered trail, through the quiet and ominous woods. Noah felt relief when they reached its end and stepped out onto a clearing. There, they stopped to rest and listen to the soothing voices of crickets and frogs, the few remaining residents of summer.

"My village is there," said Taman, pointing across the valley to the edge of another forest, where a cluster of lights sparkled like stars on Earth.

They walked beside a noisy stream that cut through the short, rough grass of the valley as they made their way to Taman's home. Behind them, Stissing Mountain was a purple shadow, backed by streaks of magenta left over from the sunset. Overhead, a sliver of new moon had risen along with Venus and Jupiter. By the time they crossed a wooden footbridge leading into the small village, Noah felt as if he were sleepwalking. Smoke rose through the rooftops of the dwellings they passed. When they arrived at a long, rectangular shaped house, Taman stopped.

"This is my home," he said, smiling.

They walked past the house to a small thatched hut, surrounded by trees, a short distance away. Taman opened the hut's door, and a rush of warmth greeted them. Inside, a pretty round-faced girl about Noah's age stood across from them by a fireplace built into the hut's wall. Taman introduced his daughter Ayanna who smiled warmly. He then nodded to her and without speaking, she picked up a basket and left her father and Noah to their dinner.

"This dwelling was built by my eldest son. He is a few years older than you. He is away now, learning about farming from one of our new neighbors. Perhaps one day you will meet him."

Noah had trouble keeping his eyes open while he and Taman ate bowls of steaming bean and corn stew. After they'd eaten, Taman gave Noah a sleeping mat and blanket before walking to the hut's entrance.

"Can you tell me what year it is?" Noah asked, before Taman stepped through the mat hanging over the doorway.

"The year is 1634," Taman replied.

"I have traveled back in time four hundred and fifty years?" Noah asked incredulously.

He remembered how his class had read about New York's history the year before. They had learned all about the Dutch colonies, the fur trade, and the American Indian tribes who lived in the region. How he wished he'd paid more careful attention.

"Before you leave, Taman, I have one more question. Back in the museum, do you know why the North American mammals came to life, but not the African mammals?"

"We live in North America. They are our animals. Sleep well, Noah," said Taman.

# Part Two: The Portal

# Chapter 6

One week after Noah disappeared, Tessa sat in her English class unable to write the rough draft of an essay she was supposed to be working on. She had no idea how anyone could be expected to concentrate on schoolwork after what had just happened. Since vacation was only two weeks away and there was still a lot of work to be done, school administrators had decided not to give any students even a day off. Instead, they had set up a guidance center in one of the classrooms where students could go to speak with counselors about Noah's disappearance.

Looking around her English class, Tessa saw that many other students, including Noah's friend Miguel, were also distracted. Some were gazing out the window with sad looks on their faces, while others were leaning their heads on their arms. Miguel, a loud-mouth who joked around a lot, had barely uttered a word since the field trip. Joshua too had found little to say during the past week. Tessa wished he would talk to her about what had happened because even though she only just met Noah, she too felt devastated.

"If anyone would like some help with their writing, please let me know," Mr. Cohen said in a gentle voice. No one took him up on his offer.

For such a quiet and unassuming person, Noah's absence sure left the school feeling empty and hollow. That morning, Tessa had walked into a restroom to find a girl named Keira in tears. Someone had whispered that she had just become Noah's girlfriend, but Tessa was sure that was not true. Even kids who didn't know Noah at all were upset. Daniela and her crew, for example, were making and distributing fliers which they decorated with their signature hearts. Daniela had even asked Tessa if she wanted to help them.

In the brief time they'd known each other, Tessa felt that she'd established a bond with Noah. And she had so few bonds these days that each one was a treasure she couldn't afford to lose. Now, Noah's disappearance mingled with the loss of her parents and sister. As she looked out the window, tears came to her eyes. She didn't want anyone to see her crying. After wiping off her glasses, she turned back to her computer and squinted intently at its screen.

Tessa remembered how she'd promised Noah that she didn't think he was crazy. But the professionals investigating the case were now saying that he had left the museum in a state of "psychological distress." They reached this conclusion after finding Noah's belongings in the museum and retrieving his phone calls and text messages off his computer. Still, Tessa firmly believed Noah had been fine and that something otherworldly was happening. She was the only one who felt sure that he was still somewhere within the museum.

The search for Noah was moved out into the city and its surrounding areas; and the museum, which had been closed, was reopened. Tessa wished someone in authority would listen to her and that they would continue their search there. She tried speaking about this to both her counselor and Noah's teacher, Ms. Rebecca, but they reacted as if she too were experiencing psychological stress.

"Tessa, we need to let the professionals do their work." Her counselor had looked her in the eye and spoken slowly and firmly.

Tessa had always been an intuitive and observant girl and often noticed or sensed things before others did. It was she who first reported her seatmate's absence at the end of the school field trip. So why wouldn't anyone listen to her now? As she tried to focus her attention on her assignment, a thought occurred to her. She owed it to Noah to try and convince his parents that they must continue searching for him within the museum.

"You have ten more minutes. These rough drafts are due tomorrow afternoon. If you do not finish them in class, then you are to complete them for homework," said Mr. Cohen, walking around the room glancing at computer screens.

After writing one more sentence, Tessa saved and closed her document. Then, making sure Mr. Cohen was not looking in her direction, she typed out a message to Joshua. He replied right away with the Bradburys' address.

When school let out, instead of getting on the bus to the depot, Tessa rode one of the institute's transports to the Bradburys' apartment building. When she arrived, she walked to the front door and pressed the call button to their apartment.

"May I help you?" a woman's voice sounded through an intercom.

"My name is Tessa, and I go to school with Noah. I would like to speak with his parents," she replied into a speaker.

A buzzer sounded to let Tessa enter the building. She rode an elevator up to the second floor, where she found Noah's mother standing in a doorway. Looking past her, Tessa saw that the apartment was a mess. All kinds of things—clothing, shoes, games, and books—were scattered everywhere. Noah's mother, who was home alone, motioned for her to step inside. After picking a tennis racket up off a chair and putting it on the floor, Tessa sat down. Mrs. Bradbury sat on the couch across from her, among piles of papers.

"So, were you a friend of Noah's?" Mrs. Bradbury asked her.

"Yes, but, well, we have only just become friends," replied Tessa who was alarmed by Mrs. Bradbury's use of the past tense.

"That must mean you did not know him well," Mrs. Bradbury responded almost matter-of-factly.

"Well, even though we just met, even though our friendship is just beginning, I feel as if I know him pretty well," asserted Tessa.

"They are telling me he may have been ill. They are implying that he may have been unhappy and run away. Did you know that?" asked Mrs. Bradbury in a manner that Tessa imagined was not that of her usual self.

"Mrs. Bradbury, I don't believe Noah ran away. I was with him, and he did not seem emotionally troubled at all."

"You may call me Joanne," said Noah's mother whose manner suddenly softened. "Would you like a cup of tea?"

"Yes, that would be nice."

While Joanne made tea, Tessa examined what she assumed were some of Noah's belongings scattered on the floor. She picked up a sand-colored rock with a white stripe running through its middle, a miniature microscope, and what looked to be an ancient shark's tooth. She looked through the books on the couch. They were mostly science and science fiction stories. Among them, she found the book *A Wrinkle in Time*. It was a beautiful old hardcover with the most amazing illustrations. The book was one of her favorites, and she had read it twice on her computer, though without any pictures. When Noah's mother returned with tea, Tessa was still looking at it.

"That was Noah's favorite. Would you like to borrow it?" asked Joanne, holding two teacups.

"Oh, I've read it already, but thank you," said Tessa.

She put the book down and walked over to a painting of a spring landscape. In it, a couple walked along a country road bordered by pink and white flowering trees.

"That's just beautiful! I love spring trees." Tessa showed Joanne the tree on her handbag.

"It was painted a long time ago by one of Noah's great-great-grandfathers," said Joanne, placing the teacups on the oak table.

"Noah told me about him. I've always wanted to be an artist. But now I'm also interested in medicine."

"I think it's possible to do both. Noah's sister says she wants to paint portraits of animals and become a veterinarian," said Joanne, smiling.

"I hope your daughter will be able to do both," said Tessa, looking away. "Is she here?"

"Madeleine has been staying with her grandparents. One day you will meet her," Joanne assured both herself and Tessa.

As they sat at the oak table sipping their tea, Tessa described how polite Noah had been, how he had let her sit in his seat on the bus, and how he had picked her purse up off the floor, even though she had been rude to him. She told his mother that while walking together to the museum's cafeteria, he had listened to her complain about her foster mother. Tessa said she felt sure Noah would have confided in her if he too had been unhappy.

"Did you know that Noah thought he had seen some display animals come to life in the museum?" asked Tessa.

"Yes, I heard he had been hallucinating."

"Well, maybe they weren't hallucinations. Maybe Noah did see them come to life. Some things can't be explained by logic alone. I think the police need to be told to keep searching the museum," Tessa finally told Mrs. Bradbury.

After she had spoken up, Tessa felt self-conscious about how she had sounded. Did Mrs. Bradbury now feel she was listening to a crazy girl? Tessa knew she looked tired and that there were dark half circles beneath her eyes.

"The police have searched every corner of the museum using robotic canines and special camera equipment. They firmly believe Noah left the museum," Joanne told her.

"But they're wrong!" Tessa said, without meaning to raise her voice. "In that story, the father has vanished," she continued, gesturing to the book both she and Noah loved.

"The kids meet a group of aliens who help them find him on another planet, in another realm. Maybe something like that has happened."

"That book is a work of fiction," Mrs. Bradbury explained, sounding a bit alarmed. "The best way we can help Noah is to take care of ourselves and allow the police to do their work," she said in a softer voice with compassion.

Tessa nodded her head in agreement. For the rest of their visit, they discussed neutral topics, such as Tessa's interest in art and the books they'd both read. When it was time for her to leave, Tessa called for an institute transport to bring her to the bus.

While riding the bus back to her neighborhood's depot, Tessa worried about the impression she'd made. She didn't want Noah's mother to think of her as a sickly, troubled girl. Having been unable to convince her that Noah was still somewhere in the museum, Tessa would now have to find a way to search for him there herself. Since she was not strong enough to work her way through the museum alone, she would have to ask Joshua to help her. As Noah's closest friend, she was almost, but not quite, sure that he would.

When Tessa arrived at the apartment building where she lived, she found her foster mother sitting on its front steps chatting with neighborhood women. As Tessa walked up the steps to the building, past the gathered group of women, she heard her loathsome foster mother whisper, "I ought to drown that one." The woman was still furious with her for going on the school field trip, when she was told to stay home and clean the apartment.

"Looks like you already might have," said a woman, chuckling.

"That girl is helping you in all kinds of ways, not the least of which is by contributing to your rent," someone else snarled. Though she was grateful to whoever had spoken up on her behalf, Tessa knew that the comment would only increase her foster mother's wrath.

Every time Tessa disobeyed her foster mother's orders, the horrible woman gave her more chores to do. When Tessa complained to her doctor about this, the doctor called the woman to explain that Tessa's illness made it dangerous for her to overexert herself. But the woman ignored the doctor and continued giving her more work. Tessa begged her caseworker at social services to find her a different home, but the social worker told her that finding a new placement would be difficult.

"Even though the virus you contracted is no longer contagious, people are still afraid to take in a child who has been exposed to it," the caseworker explained. "I believe your foster mother is a good person. She has provided care for many sick and disabled children. I know the neighborhood she lives in is not great, but even still, Tessa, you are lucky to have received a placement with her."

The caseworker was wrong, Tessa was not lucky, and she and her foster mother continued to clash. Tessa knew it was unlikely she would survive much beyond young adulthood. All she wanted was to find peace in whatever time she had left. She wanted to spend it reading, learning, doing artwork, and getting to know and be herself.

Walking into the apartment, Tessa found her foster siblings stretched out like stray cats all over the small living room. Some were watching television and others were playing games. The tiny apartment had no climate control like the ones at the institute, and it was always hot. Its walls were paper thin and sound from neighboring units constantly seeped in. The two boys would stay up half the night giggling over what they could hear.

As she walked through the room, the oldest girl in the apartment, their foster mother's favorite, looked up at her from her perch on the armrest of the couch.

"You'll need to clean the kitchen and both the boys' and girls' dormitories tonight," she said. "When you clean ours, remember what I always have to tell you. Don't touch my bedding or clothes. I don't want to catch what you have."

There always seemed to be at least someone in the apartment with a fever or a runny nose. Tessa's illness was probably the only one that was no longer contagious. She would never have been placed in a foster home if it had been. Still, she sometimes preferred to let people believe otherwise. Like a cat's sharp claws, the threat of it offered protection.

Before going to bed, Tessa managed to clean up the kitchen, wash dishes, and wipe down the counters and cabinets. The bedrooms would have to wait. She hoped no one would notice and that she would be left alone until morning. Unable to sleep, she lay awake for hours listening to the wheezing and snoring in the beds around her. Her mind would not give her any rest. Sneaking into the museum would be very risky and asking Joshua to help her do so might not be fair. But there wasn't any other way.

Tessa knew Joshua would probably agree to help her and that she could trust him. But she wasn't sure it was even right to ask him. He loved being at the institute, and she did not want to get him into trouble and jeopardize his ability to go to school there. Nor did she wish to endanger her placement there. Even if a lot of the kids there shunned her, attending school at the institute was the only secure and good thing in her life.

Tessa looked up at the clock. She read its glowing numbers and panicked over how late it was. She knew she would never fall asleep until she sent Joshua a message proposing her plan. She got out of bed, found the computer tablet loaned to her by the institute, and brought it out into the living room. The living room's window was usually locked shut, adding to a feeling of incarceration and claustrophobia, but tonight it had been left open. Tessa pushed it up and crawled out onto the fire escape.

On the street below, people were singing and dancing, though it was well past midnight. The December night was warm and muggy, and overhead an almost full moon, easily mistaken for a searchlight, beamed down through a humid haze. Tessa looked up at it imploringly before composing her message. After it was sent, she sat waiting, listening to the music. The popular love song was suddenly interrupted by loud, angry shouts. Quickly, Tessa crawled back into the apartment. She was peering through the window, watching people run through the streets, when the musical notes on her tablet sounded. Fearing the noise would wake someone up, she climbed back out onto the fire escape to read the message.

"When would you like to go?" Joshua asked.

"Tomorrow morning," she typed back.

"Are you crazy? We need a little time to plan for this, Tessa!"

"Please, we don't have time to plan. We can't wait."

"All right, if you believe we can find him. I will see you tomorrow morning at the depot," came the reply.

Elated and over the moon, Tessa quietly crept back into the living room. She was about to return to the girls' dormitory, when she spotted her foster mother's purse sitting on a table. Steadying herself, she reached inside and searched until she found the plastic money card. Hiding it inside her tablet, she quickly returned to her bed in the dormitory. Soon the sun would rise, and the apartment would be full of activity, but at the moment, everyone around her was sound asleep.

# Chapter 7

"It's time to get up." A voice woke Noah from a dream. In the dream, he had been walking on a wooded trail when someone called out to him. When he turned around, he saw that it was Tessa, but before he could speak to her, Taman had woken him up.

"We have a lot of work to do, Noah. We must prepare you for your journey," Taman called to him from the hut's doorway.

Taman tossed a fur wrap and leather pack onto the floor. Noah looked at them both and then around the hut in confusion. For a moment, he had forgotten where he was. Then he remembered the events of the day before. None of it had been a dream after all.

Just before sunrise, he and Taman left the village and retraced their steps of the previous night. They hiked across the valley and through the woods, making their way back toward the mountains. The rising sun burned off the early morning dampness and chill, and by midmorning the October day turned into a warm and summery one.

Looking at the surrounding autumn landscape, Noah recalled how he'd longed for this moment while standing by the diorama of Stissing Mountain in the museum. As he and Taman hiked along the trail, Noah learned that the world he had entered, though beautiful, was not without problems. Taman began to tell him about new settlers who were arriving in the river valley each year. Some made for friendly neighbors, but others were aggressive, imposing their ways on everyone else and demanding rights to land and hunting territory. Taman warned him that he was to travel through some conflicted regions, and that he must always remain aware of his surroundings.

As they walked, Taman taught Noah how to spot signs that indicated the presence or recent passage of a person or animal. They looked for footprints, broken branches, and displaced rocks.

"We just missed a passing deer," Taman said, stopping at a steaming pile of newly left deer droppings. Noah grimaced and turned away.

Moments later, it was Noah who spotted several tufts of coarse black and white fur on the ground beneath a spiky branched bush.

"After shedding old fur in the fall, skunks grow new fur to keep them warm throughout the winter," explained Taman. "This fur was probably left here weeks ago. That is good, since we would rather not meet a skunk."

Taman also taught Noah techniques for remaining undetected while traveling through the woods. Noah learned how to step noiselessly over leaves and twigs; how to avoid leaving footprints by stepping down on his heel and rolling his foot onto its side; and how to disappear behind a tree, by sucking in his abdomen and standing still and tall.

Along the trail, they passed several different species of Northeastern trees, whose leaves dropped continually to the ground and collected in piles underfoot. Noah shuffled through them, stopping now and then to pick one up. There were yellow leaves from hickory, birch, and oak trees and dark purple ones from ash trees. Others were green with red veins, and yellow and red spots. These fell from sycamore and maple trees and resembled the classic fall leaves Noah had seen on his computer. Noah was admiring one when a shrill cry sounded overhead. He looked up to see a winged creature darting across their path.

"Most of our songbirds have flown south, but others remain with us," said Taman.

"In my world, many species of birds are protected in the tree sanctuaries. But there are some who survive outside. In the city, there are a lot of feral pigeons and sparrows," Noah told him.

Taman wore a solemn expression but said nothing.

At midday, they stopped to rest and eat the smoked deer meat and flatbread that Taman had brought for them. The salty meat, which Noah now understood was real, made him thirsty and he drank heavily from his water flask. Looking through the items that Taman had put in his pack, Noah found a steel knife, a rock, and long strips of leather. He had no idea what he would use them for. While examining his new belongings, a loud caw sounded overhead. On a nearby tree, a large black bird peered down at them.

"That crow! He must be the same one who flew from the diorama into the museum. I think he is following me," Noah said, standing up.

Taman squinted as he looked up at the fierce-looking creature. "Crows are intelligent birds. They are messengers and bring good luck. It is believed that they were the only creature to have survived the great flood of long ago."

"Do you mean the flood that's talked about in the Bible? In the story of Noah, he builds an ark to save the animals from that flood. Did the animal spirits think I could help them because my name is Noah?"

"I believe the animals chose you because of who you are. I do not know the story of that other Noah. Perhaps you will tell it to me one day," said Taman. "But now there is a story I wish to tell you. It is the story of the Great Oak or the Grandmother Oak, as she is called by many."

The crow flew away, and Noah became Taman's only listener.

"Long ago, a group of people fled their homeland and wandered lost for many years. They traveled across Earth's harshest terrains and knew many hardships, those of hunger, thirst, and sickness. After two generations passed, the Great Spirit led the people into a new land, one filled with abundance and beauty. There, a baby girl was the first to be born on its soil.

"When the girl grew to be a young woman, she met a young man who became her true love. The couple bore a son, but to their great sadness, the baby did not survive. Heartbroken, the young woman never had another child. Instead, she became a healer who helped other babies live and other mothers give birth. Even as an old woman, she continued to help people overcome sickness. When her mate left this world, the Great Spirit blessed her with a renewed and long life, transforming her into a beautiful white oak tree. Only then was she able to bear more children."

"For all the years since, the Grandmother Oak has replenished her forests, while protecting and healing her lands, and providing food and shelter for many creatures. Though she remains hidden, she too is now in danger. The old trees are being cut down for their wood. Some believe that the Grandmother Oak is ready to leave this world. It is said she is tired and wishes to reunite with her mate and son. Before she leaves our Earth, you must find her and bring one of her offspring back to your own time."

Noah immediately thought of his mother's oak table, the heirloom that brought his family together. Though he understood that a tree, like the one Taman described, had been destroyed to make it, he still loved the table. It too was a family member, who gave him a feeling of home and security.

"We must be going," announced Taman. "We still have a ways to travel."

For the rest of the afternoon, they walked mostly in silence, each lost in his own thoughts. They arrived at the first foothill of the mountain range just before sunset. After choosing a spot for their camp, Taman prepared a banked fire. Noah lay down on the hard ground beside the snapping flames. While the sun set, a crescent moon rose in the darkening sky. In the surrounding distance, the mountains appeared purple and blue against the red-streaked horizon. After the long day of hiking, Noah fell quickly to sleep.

The following morning, Taman assigned Noah the task of finding water. Carrying two pouches, both made from the stomachs of deer, Noah hiked through the woods toward what sounded like water gurgling over rocks. Clearing his way through an overgrown trail, he found a stream descending from the mountains. After falling in a narrow and rushing torrent, it widened and spread out over level ground.

The day, like the previous one, was unusually warm for October in the world of the past. Noah took off his outer clothing and moccasins and left them on the stream's bank. Then, wearing only his breechcloth, he tied the two pouches together, draped them over his shoulders, and waded into the water. He had never walked into a mountain stream before. The slippery rocks and swift-moving water made it hard for him to maintain his balance. He tried to step only on stones that were large and flat, but twice his foot landed on ones that were painfully sharp and jagged. It was a relief when the stream's bed deepened and he no longer had to walk. Slipping into the water, Noah swam to a large flat-topped rock at the stream's center.

Climbing onto the rock, Noah lay down on his stomach and as he had in the museum, filled his cupped hands with water. The cool, clean water tasted nothing like the bland liquid at home. Noah never imagined anything could taste so wonderful. After filling both pouches, he left them on the rock and jumped back in the stream, quenching a thirst he felt throughout his body.

Floating on his back, he felt the warm October sun on his face as he looked up at the sky and the yellow-leafed trees. He could have spent all day swimming in the stream, if not for the errand he was supposed to be running. Swimming vigorously against the current, he returned to the rock and retrieved the water pouches. Then, struggling once more over the slippery rocks, he made his way to the river bank where he dressed quickly and found the trail back to camp. When he arrived, Taman looked at him sternly but said nothing about Noah's lateness.

"We will spend the afternoon searching for food," Taman announced, interrupting their uncomfortable silence. "You are forbidden from harming any animal or person in this world. That means, you will not be able to hunt for meat."

"I don't think I would be good at hunting anyway," Noah replied, somewhat timidly.

After setting up snares for small game, Taman helped Noah search for edible plants. He showed Noah where to find nuts, berries, and roots that were safe to eat and plentiful in the region. Some of these plants were easily confused with poisonous ones. It was crucial that Noah learn to identify them correctly by the shape and color of their leaves, and by the way those leaves grew around their stems. Since it was autumn, there were few fresh, leafy greens to be found. But Noah did find plenty of chestnuts, a few starchy roots, and some wild crab apples that he and Taman ate, along with their flatbread and smoked deer meat, for dinner.

That night, the weather changed drastically. In the morning, there was a biting chill in the air, and Taman told Noah they would spend the day building shelters, one for each of them. Noah was excited about doing so as he'd always loved building forts. When he was a little kid, he would make tents in his bedroom out of sheets, and when his mother allowed him to, he would drape the quilt his great-grandmother had made over the oak table. Crawling into the newly created space, he would eat a snack while reading a book. There he would remain, until one of his parents would ask in an exaggerated voice, "Noah, where are you?"

After collecting sturdy tree branches, Taman and Noah began to build their shelters. They each tied several large branches together using leather strips, like the ones Noah found in his pack, to form long triangular-shaped frames. The ends of the branches were dug into the ground and secured in place with rocks. The sides of the shelters were then were filled in with woven branches, pine needles, grass, and leaves.

The two shelters were finished just before darkness settled in over the mountains. As they sat by the fire eating the remainder of the deer meat Taman had brought, Noah admired their day's work. The dwellings looked like nests an animal or a bird might make. They seemed sturdy enough and blended in well with the environment. It would soon prove that the effort it took to make them had been worth it. Throughout their stay in the mountains, the dwellings would keep them warm, dry, and safe on the cold and rainy autumn nights to come.

The next day, when they returned to check on the snares Taman had set, they found that a raccoon and two rabbits had been caught. In Noah's world, it was a crime to kill most animals. He remembered how as a kid, he had played with rabbits at the institute. Though plentiful here, back in his world most rabbits now lived in the conservatories. After looking down at one of the small, broken creatures, Noah looked up to find Taman watching him. Though Noah hadn't said anything, he knew that Taman had seen and felt his disapproval.

While the rabbits roasted, drizzling an aromatic fat onto the crackling fire, Noah felt a gnawing ache in his stomach. Though he felt guilty, when they were ready to be eaten Noah was so hungry that he ignored his conscience and devoured the meat.

"Thank you, Taman," he said softly while cleaning his hands, rubbing them onto the soil before dipping them in a bowl of water. Taman looked up and nodded.

That evening, as they sat by the fire, Noah looked up at the vast dome of stars overhead. Only in the museum's Planetarium had he seen such a sight. He found the Big and Little Dippers and spotted a fiery bird, darting across the sky. Taman pointed to a bright star and explained that when facing it, one was facing north. He told Noah that the North Star could help anyone find their way home. Within this world of vast wilderness, it was easy to get lost.

When Noah crawled into his fort that night, he continued looking at a patch of starry sky through a gap in the roof. While waiting for sleep, Noah thought about how his wordless reaction to the animals caught in the snares must have offended Taman. Noah hadn't meant to be offensive; he just couldn't help how he'd felt. The fact was that even though he and Taman both lived on Earth, they were from two vastly different worlds.

# Chapter 8

After making himself breakfast and a bagged lunch, Joshua headed to the bus depot as he always did. There he met Tessa. Instead of taking their regular bus to the institute, they used their student transportation passes to board a bus that was heading into New York City. Once in the city, they used their passes again to hop on the subway train that brought them right up to the American Museum of Natural History.

"Are you with a school group?" a cashier at the museum's ticket counter asked them.

"Our school gave us permission to spend the day here to do some research and drawings for our science project," Tessa politely informed the cashier, with a confidence Joshua envied, as she handed the young woman a money card.

"I see," said the cashier, who regarded them both with suspicion. Still, the cashier swiped the money card and then handed Tessa two tickets. Joshua looked at Tessa out of the corner of his eye. Though he was relieved, he couldn't believe how effort-lessly Tessa had just pulled that off.

"Where did you get that money card?" Joshua whispered.

"I found it in my foster mother's purse." Tessa looked at him and smiled.

"You stole your foster mother's money card?" he asked incredulously.

"I don't see it as stealing. My foster mother owes me money. She's been keeping the allowance that the foster care agency gives me. She says I owe it to her for all the extra attention she has to give me."

"Why don't you report her to someone at the agency?"

"I have, Joshua. I have told both my caseworker and my doctor about her. Neither one of them has done anything. They tell me I am lucky she's agreed to take me in because most people don't want to deal with someone who's had, 'the virus.'"

"You know, I should probably buy my own ticket," said Joshua.

"No, I am the one who asked you to come," she insisted. "I'm the only one who might get in trouble."

"All right, fine!" Joshua didn't want to argue about it. Besides, tickets were expensive, and it was true after all that Tessa had begged him for his help.

While they stood in the Theodore Roosevelt Rotunda try-ing to decide what to do, Joshua suggested that they split up. He wanted to search for a secluded spot where they could hide out while the museum closed. Tessa's illness would not allow her to walk as quickly or as much as he could, and he figured he would have to cover a lot of territory in order to find a suitable place. Thankfully, Tessa agreed to this plan and asked Joshua to walk her over to the Hall of Biodiversity on the first floor. There, she took out a sketchbook from her cloth bag, sat down by the African rainforest, and began sketching the Siberian tiger.

To avoid being questioned by security guards, Joshua spent the entire morning tailing one middle school group while searching for a place to hide. By noon, having not found one he was comfortable with, he reluctantly returned to the first floor where he'd agreed to meet Tessa for lunch.

"That's amazing!" he exclaimed when Tessa showed him her drawing.

"It's not finished yet. Let's buy lunch in the café. My treat!"

"Thanks, but I brought my lunch," Joshua declined, firmly.

"I did too, but we can save them for later."

"Tessa, you cannot keep using that money card."

"Fine! This will be the last time," Tessa sighed.

At the café, despite his continued protests, Tessa bought them both protein burgers, potato fries, and orange-flavored vitamin drinks. Joshua sat across from her at the end of a long table and, though he felt guilty about it, enjoyed his food. While looking around the room at some of the families who were with kids who also should have been in school, he had an idea.

"I will be right back; wait here," he told Tessa.

Leaving the visitors' café, Joshua walked over to check out the school lunchrooms where several groups were gathered. Although it was possible to hide beneath a table there, Joshua was sure that later the entire area would be cleaned and checked. He walked back to the food counter and while peering into the kitchen area behind it, a security guard whom he hadn't seen, called out to him.

"Are you looking for something?" she inquired.

"No, I just..." Joshua anxiously stumbled over his words.

"Isn't that your group over there?" she asked, pointing him in the direction of a school lunchroom where the middle school group he'd been following earlier was assembled. After the security guard led him to the group, she walked away. Quickly, Joshua ran back to Tessa in the visitors' café.

"We need to be very careful from now on. One of the guards just noticed me," he told her breathlessly.

Cautiously, the two brought their empty food trays and drink containers to the recycling bins. After putting his paper tray in one of the bins, Joshua stood and stared at them. There were two containers for paper, one for glass and another for biodegradables. He was sure that he could fit inside one.

"Are you ready?" Tessa asked him. "I want to go back to the first floor to finish my sketch."

For the rest of the afternoon, as Joshua continued his search, he tried to remain inconspicuous by blending in with different school groups as they wandered through the museum's halls. When a voice over the intercom announced that the museum would soon be closing, he hurried to the Hall of Biodiversity where he found Tessa impatiently waiting for him by the tiger.

"What took you so long?" she asked him.

"I'm sorry! Look, we're going to have to hide in the recycling bins in the visitors' café. There just isn't anywhere else," Joshua informed her.

"That's disgusting!" Tessa objected. "And what happens if later, while we are in them, someone wants to roll them out onto the street for recycling pickup?"

"Then we'll be put out with them. It's just a risk we have to take."

"Can't we hide in a bathroom?"

"I think the recycling bins are our best choice."

While the kitchen area of the café was being cleaned, Joshua and Tessa crept into the recycling section like two shadowy scavengers. There, Joshua helped Tessa climb into one of the two paper containers, before he climbed into the other. They did so just in time. Workers entered the area to stack chairs and vacuum the floor. Joshua and Tessa remained still and barely breathed as the workers laughed and told jokes.

Later, after the café's staff had gone home, they continued to remain calm, when they heard a security guard and dog approach. Joshua's heart beat in his chest as he listened to the dog whining and sniffing. Perhaps the dog was unable to detect their scent over the garbage, or maybe he did sense them, but the guard assumed that he was whining because of the food. Either way, it was a relief when the guard led the greatest threat to their discovery away. Had the dog been one of the new robotic ones, he and Tessa most surely would have been discovered.

While Tessa slept, Joshua, who was too uncomfortable to sleep, remained awake and alert, listening for other worrisome sounds. After it had been quiet for almost an hour, he cautiously climbed out of his bin and woke Tessa. They were both stiff and achy, and wanted to wash off the sticky residue from the paper food packaging and trays. After stretching their legs and using the restrooms, they walked up a flight of stairs to the first floor.

"We need to go look at the mountain lion's diorama," said Tessa.

"Why exactly do we need to do that?"

"Because of what Noah said he had seen. We will walk by them quickly," she promised.

Walking side by side, Tessa and Joshua slowly entered the Hall of North American Mammals which, as on the night Noah was there, was lit by eerie, orange security lights. As they walked to the end of the hall, all around them the animals remained still and lifeless. When they arrived at the cougar's diorama, they stopped and stared. Only the male cougar, who turned his head to regard them, was present.

"So, Noah wasn't hallucinating," Joshua heard himself say.

"I never thought he was. We need to find her," Tessa replied.

"Tessa, I don't want to go searching for a mountain lion."

"But that is what we came here to do," Tessa informed him.

"I thought we came here to search for Noah."

"The cougar knows where he is. She will bring us to him."

They found the tawny-coated cat in the Hall of Biodiversity, lying near the encased Siberian tiger whose portrait Tessa had drawn. The cougar looked up at them before rising to her feet and sauntering in the direction of the Hall of North American Forests. She stopped, turned around, and look directly at Tessa as if asking her to follow.

The cougar led them through the Halls of Biodiversity and North American Forests and into the Hall of New York State. Each time Tessa stopped to catch her breath, the cat waited patiently for her. When they arrived at the diorama called *An October Afternoon Near Stissing Mountain*, both Joshua and Tessa stopped and stared. Everything within the diorama—a little red fox, geese, and blue jays—had come back to life.

"I think we should call someone and tell them about this," Joshua said.

"No one will believe us. Noah is in there, and we have to find him," Tessa replied.

The cougar, who had been standing quietly nearby, strolled into the now glassless display case, terrifying the little red fox who bolted away. The cat waited on the dirt path, looking back at them.

"We need to keep following her, Joshua," Tessa told him.

"I am not going in there," he replied adamantly.

"Let's just look around to see if Noah's there. We'll be quick," Tessa tried to encourage him.

"No, Tessa!" Joshua answered firmly.

"Fine, I will go by myself. Will you please hold my bag for me?"

"I'm not going to hold your bag for you. I don't think you should go in there."

Joshua couldn't believe Tessa would even consider doing something so reckless. He wished she would listen to him. Instead, she let out an exasperated sigh and placed her bag on the bench in front of the diorama. Joshua looked on with dismay as the frail but determined girl stepped into the now open display case. After looking around at the view, she turned back to him and smiled.

"Joshua, I knew it all along. This diorama does lead to a whole other world, and it is such a beautiful one. Oh look!" she exclaimed.

Something, Joshua did not know what, had caught Tessa's attention. He stood there and watched as she walked to the right along the trail and out of view.

"Tessa!" he yelled.

Only when she did not answer did he try to follow her into the diorama. The glass, however, had reappeared, blocking him from entering. He shouted and hit it with both hands, but it was of no use. He waited for Tessa to return for who knew how long. When she did not appear, he took her cloth bag and made his way in a frightened daze back to the museum's main entrance.

At first, he didn't know whom to call for help. He was afraid to call the police, and he did not want to call and terrify his mother. Then Joshua remembered Tessa telling him that her teacher, despite his bullish demeanor, was someone who genuinely cared. He took Tessa's computer out of her bag and found Mr. Gerard's phone number in its address book.

The teacher arrived about an hour later, in the company of someone who looked to be either a police officer or a security guard. The man unlocked the museum's front door and when he and Mr. Gerard stepped inside, Joshua became overwhelmed by emotion and filled with relief.

"May I speak to him privately?" Joshua heard Mr. Gerard ask the official.

The man nodded, and Mr. Gerard led Joshua to an area by the Christmas tree.

"What's going on?" Mr. Gerard asked Joshua.

Though he never expected anyone to believe his story, he still had trouble believing it himself, Joshua told Tessa's teacher everything that had happened since they left for the museum on the morning of the previous day.

"That is a hard story to believe," Mr. Gerard sighed and shook his head.

"It's the truth," Joshua replied.

Over the next several days Joshua tried to remain calm while being questioned by police, psychiatrists, and social workers.

He followed Mr. Gerard's advice and told authorities the truth, in its most simple form, about what had happened. Joshua explained to them that he had agreed to help Tessa search for Noah in the museum, and that while doing so, they became separated from one another. He was asked many unfair questions that were confusing and sounded more like accusations.

"Were you jealous of Noah's new friendship with Tessa?" a social worker asked in a syrupy voice.

"Of course not," he replied.

"Did you tell Tessa to take her foster mother's money card?" a police officer asked firmly.

"No, I told her she was wrong to take it," Joshua asserted.

"Why were you in possession of Tessa's handbag?" asked another officer.

"She left it on the bench," Joshua answered truthfully.

"Didn't the institute provide you with your own tablet?"

"Yes, but I left it at home."

"Is that why you took Tessa's?"

"I didn't take Tessa's tablet."

"No? Didn't you use her tablet to place a call to her teacher?"

"Yes, but that was how I got his number."

Joshua tried to answer everyone's questions honestly. But he had to be careful. It was as if they were all trying to catch him in a lie.

Despite protests from Mr. Gerard, Ms. Rebecca, Miguel, and many fellow students, Joshua was asked not to return to the institute's school, even though there were only a few days left before the winter holidays. He wondered if an institute kid would have been treated in the same way had he or she been in his place.

Since enrolling at the institute, Joshua had become excited about learning. He had even planned on becoming a scientist and wanted to choose a specific area to research and write about, just like Noah's parents had. When Joshua found out where his new school assignment was to be, he felt hopeless. He knew about the school. It was crowded, with angry, unmotivated kids who were expected to sit at their desks all day, which they never did, and read boring essays meant to prepare them for stupid tests.

After school, instead of running track, he would have to meet with his court-appointed lawyer and psychiatrist. As the primary suspect in the disappearance of his two friends, Joshua's entire life changed overnight. He now felt so alone. His life became a lie, and he felt helpless as others steered him toward a future and identity that had nothing to do with who he was.

# Chapter 9

For as long as she could remember, Tessa had felt a kinship with cats. She had always loved them, and they loved her back. She could win over even the snarliest, most tangled up knot of a creature. After a few softly spoken words, the hissing and growling of even those most hopelessly feral would cease, and she would be allowed to approach.

When Tessa stepped into the diorama and saw that the cougar had been joined by two cubs, she couldn't help herself. It was as if an invisible magnet drew her toward them. Since her bond with cats had only been established with the smallest of the feline species, Tessa approached them with caution.

The cougar, having finished her job of leading Tessa into the diorama, was now lying down just off the trail, while her cubs played around her. When Tessa sat down nearby, the male cub ran up to her. Cautiously, Tessa scratched behind his ears and he plopped down beside her and began to purr. With a lazy indifference, the cougar watched as her second offspring, a baby female, bounced up to Tessa as well.

"Joshua! You have to come and see this," Tessa called out, but Joshua didn't answer.

Gently, Tessa pushed the cubs away and stood up. Her attention had been so fixed on the cougars that she hadn't even noticed her surroundings. She looked out at the tree-filled landscape. As she had suspected, the museum did lead to another realm.

"Joshua, can you hear me?" called Tessa, as she made her way back to where the diorama's entrance had been.

But the entrance was no longer there. Tessa ran her hands along the wall of rock trying to find it, but all she could find was a small indentation where the diorama was supposed to be. She began to claw at the granite wall, but it would not yield, and all she managed to do was break her fingernails and scrape up her hands.

What kind of a place had she entered into? There were no people to be seen anywhere. Suddenly, Tessa recalled the television show that her foster siblings liked to watch. In it, a group of people were imprisoned on a beautiful yet hostile island. What if the realm she now found herself in was a similar place?

"Joshua, where are you? You need to help me!" Tessa screamed.

The cougar, as if to remind Tessa that she was not alone, cried out to her. Tessa turned to see the cat and her two cubs looking at her. As the cougar had done back in the museum, she seemed to be asking Tessa to follow her. Perhaps the cat was going to lead Tessa to Noah.

The diorama's sun was about to disappear behind the mountains. Soon this strange and foreign world would grow dark.

Tessa had no choice but to step in line behind the two cubs as they bounded after their mother down the mountain path to the woods below. Though she was weak and exhausted, Tessa struggled to keep up with them.

At the bottom of the slope, they arrived at an intersection where the path joined what looked to be a well-used road. There, Tessa collapsed beneath a pine tree. The cougar waited for Tessa to get back on her feet, but Tessa was unable to. She looked at Tessa, sadly it seemed, before turning away and walking into the woods with her cubs. The family of cats disappeared, and as the light diminished, Tessa, as she had always done when frightened or upset, closed her eyes, and curled up into herself.

"Who are you?" A girl's voice startled her.

Opening her eyes, Tessa looked up and squinted. Walking toward her on the road was a girl who looked to be about Tessa's age, leading a supply-laden horse.

"I am looking for a boy. His name is Noah," Tessa called back.

"The boy is here. But how did you get here?" asked the girl as she walked up to Tessa.

"I followed a mountain lion into the diorama, and she left me here."

"The boy Noah, is with my father. The doorway was supposed to close after his arrival," said the girl, who looked at Tessa in disbelief.

"Doorway to where? Where are we?" asked Tessa, wrapping her arms around herself.

In the fading light, Tessa noticed that a fine powder was rubbing off her pink and white flowered blouse onto her fingers. The substance was like the coating that rubbed off a butterfly's wing when it was not handled properly.

"Your clothes! They won't last long in our world," said the girl. The girl then took one of the packs off the horse's back and began to search through it.

Tessa's entire outfit seemed to be disintegrating. The soles of her shoes were crumbling like two stale pieces of bread, and her glasses, now soft and gelatinous, were sliding down the bridge of her nose. Though she didn't need her glasses to read, Tessa needed them to see the teaching screen at school and to identify people and objects at a distance.

"My name is Ayanna," said the girl, handing Tessa the skirt and blouse she had taken out of the pack.

"I need to find my friend who came with me to the museum. We need to go home and tell Noah's mother that he is here," said Tessa as she put the skirt and blouse on over what was left of her clothes.

"I don't know if that's possible," said Ayanna.

"I have to go home to take my medication," said Tessa whose voice rose with fear.

"We will return to my home. You may stay with my family and wait for my father. He will know why you are here," said Ayanna.

"You don't want me to stay at your home. I have an illness, and you don't want to catch it," Tessa warned her.

"Your illness cannot harm me. Like clothing, diseases from the future are not allowed into the world of the past," Ayanna replied even though she backed away in fear.

Tessa looked at Ayanna in confusion. What did the strange girl mean exactly? Had she traveled back in time?

"Even though yours may be a disease of the future, we must be careful," interrupted a boy's voice.

Tessa turned around to see the boy walking toward them on the road behind her. He was carrying a lantern that brightened the darkening landscape.

"Many new settlers have brought illness into our world from other lands. Still, our father would have you return home with us where you will remain safe. He will want to know how you came to be here," said the teenaged boy when he arrived.

The boy, a young man really, looked to be a few years older than his sister, Ayanna. Though Tessa felt somewhat frightened by his arrival, the boy had a handsome face and she could hear a sensitivity in his voice as he spoke. Night was falling, and it had become very chilly, something unfamiliar to Tessa. There seemed to be no better choice than to travel with the brother and sister to their home and await their father and Noah's return from wherever they were.

All that remained of Tessa's shoes were two small piles of sand, and since Ayanna had no shoes to offer her, Tessa walked barefoot. Without her glasses, it was hard for her to see, especially now that it was growing dark, and when she stepped on a sharp stone, she cried out.

"Elan, the horse is carrying many things, but there is still room for the girl on her back," said Ayanna.

Tessa had never seen a horse before, let alone ridden one. The animal was enormous. Elan helped lift her onto the animal's broad back. The horse didn't even seem to notice the additional weight of her small frame. Tessa wrapped her arms around the horse's neck and held on tightly as they made their way along the road. Up ahead Elan's lantern broke through the darkness that had quickly descended upon them. Despite the bumpy ride, Tessa fell asleep and did not open her eyes until Ayanna and her brother helped her into their home.

When Tessa awoke the next morning, she was lying on a mat next to the wall of a long, one-room house. At one end of the room, several women and children were sitting by a fire, eating breakfast. Tessa saw that Ayanna was among them and very bravely walked over to her.

"My name is Tessa," she said, finally introducing herself.

"This is my mother, Nora. She welcomes you to her and my father Taman's home," Ayanna replied.

The woman looked at Tessa with a solemn expression before smiling broadly and motioning for her to sit down. Ayanna told Tessa that her mother, who spoke little English, believed there was an important reason why Tessa was there.

"We told my aunts that you are an orphan girl who came to New Netherland from far away. They do not know about the doorway to the future," Ayanna whispered.

The fact that Tessa was an orphan who came from far away was, in fact, the truth, though Tessa did not tell this to Ayanna.

"I have come back to the time of New Netherland?" Tessa could not believe what Ayanna had told her.

"Yes! The doorway will not open for just anyone. As with the boy, there must be a reason why you are here," Ayanna assured her.

"The only reason I am here is to find Noah and help him come home," answered Tessa.

For the next several days, Tessa kept to herself in the long-house. Ayanna's family shared their house with the families of her mother's two younger sisters, and being among them all made Tessa long for her parents and sister.

After waking up each morning Tessa spent the day alone, sitting beneath an ash tree, looking out across the valley, waiting for Noah. She knew that she was here to help him. Still, she worried that without her medication she would become sick again. If she did, no one here would be able to help her, and she wouldn't be able to help Noah.

One morning, about a week after her arrival, she was sitting under the ash tree tracing circles on the ground with a stick, when she looked up to find Elan looking down at her. She hadn't seen him since the night of her arrival.

"Would you like to have a tour of our village?" he asked her.

Tessa would have preferred to remain by herself, but she did not want to be unfriendly to Elan the way she had been to Noah, and so she agreed to join him.

"Whenever I am angry or unhappy, I walk in the woods," Elan told her. "I look at the trees and listen to the many sounds all around me."

Tessa did not reply as she and Elan walked. Still, he continued to talk to her. He told her about the farm where he worked and about the new settler who owned it. From his homeland, the settler had brought the seeds of a tree that bore a round, red fruit that ripened during the harvest season. Two years ago, when he'd first started working for the settler farmer, Elan had helped him grow the seeds into saplings. This year, the farmer had given him some of the tree's seeds as part of his payment, and next spring Elan planned to raise saplings of his own.

"You want to build an apple orchard?" Tessa spoke for the first time. She had lifted herself up a bit out of her terrible mood.

"Yes! I will plant an apple orchard." Elan looked at her and smiled.

As they passed through the village, Elan introduced her to the people they met as the girl who was visiting from far away. They arrived at the village's farm where several children were working. Tessa watched a young girl cut a yellow, oval-shaped vegetable from its vine.

"Here we grow beans and different varieties of squash," Elan told her as they looked out over the field. "This spring in addition to the fruit trees, I hope to plant barley and oats."

"All I have ever wanted was to be an artist. But now I also wish I could help cure people of diseases," she confided.

"There is something you might like to see," Elan told her.

He brought her to a hut on the edge of the woods filled with all kinds of pottery. There were cups, plates, bowls of all sizes, and even vases for flowers. They were decorated with different designs and images and were the colors of the earth—different tones of brown, black, gray, and pale yellow.

"My mother made these," said Elan, pointing to a shelf covered with ceramics. "In a few weeks, many will be brought to a market for trading."

Tessa walked over to look at them. Among the cups and bowls was a sculpture of a mother holding a child. Tessa remembered with sadness the only piece of ceramics she had ever made, a small sculpture of a dog.

"They're beautiful," Tessa said softly.

The day after their walk, Elan returned to his work on the settler's farm. Tessa, feeling sad once more, remembered his advice and went to the woods to walk beneath the autumn trees.

There were so many different species of trees. Tessa ran her hand along the trunk of one whose bark was white and smooth, and along another whose brown bark was rough and cracked like the scaly skin of a reptile. As the fiery-colored trees dropped their leaves, the wind scattered them everywhere. The trail Tessa walked along was littered with them. Wearing the new leather shoes Ayanna's mother Nora had given her, she carefully stepped over the medley of colors and shapes, red, yellow, and purple leaves in the forms of stars, hearts, and feathers.

Among the leaves, Tessa soon discovered there were many seeds. Some of the seeds were designed like propellers and fell from the trees, spinning to the ground like ballet dancers. Other seeds were wrapped in fuzzy coats that stuck to the new leather dress Ayanna's mother had made for Tessa. There were acorns and chestnuts all over the ground. Some had smooth shells, while others had shells that were spiked like the weapons of ancient warriors. Tessa began picking many of the seeds up. She would start a collection of them. Elan had been right— while walking through the woods, her sadness went away.

On her way back to the village, Tessa arrived at the hut Elan had shown her. The door was open, and she stepped inside. Though she knew she shouldn't, she picked up one of Nora's ceramic bowls and turned it in her hands. The sound of a clearing throat startled her, and when she turned around to see Nora glaring at her, the bowl slipped from her hand and shattered on the ground. Nora took Tessa by her arm and led her back to the longhouse. Without speaking, Nora made it clear to Tessa that she was to remain there.

Sitting on her sleeping mat, Tessa listened to Nora speak angrily to Ayanna in their language. Tessa hadn't talked much to Ayanna since her first morning in the village, and now she felt sure that Ayanna and her mother would ask her to leave their home. She did not know how she would survive if they did.

"It was an accident!" Tessa wanted to yell.

Then she noticed that Ayanna was angry with her mother. When Nora left the longhouse, Ayanna immediately walked over to her.

"You must no longer wander alone. You will begin to help us prepare for the winter. We will work together," Ayanna told her. Tessa assumed that Ayanna was not happy about this arrangement.

The following morning, while Tessa helped Ayanna shake out mats, Nora interrupted them. This time, after Ayanna and her mother had spoken, Ayanna appeared to be happy. Tessa assumed that Nora must have relieved her daughter of having to watch over her. Perhaps now Tessa really would be asked to leave. Again, Tessa filled with fear, but Ayanna walked up to her excitedly.

"My mother has invited us to help her with her pottery. She said she liked how you showed interest in her work. We leave tomorrow morning and we must be ready. Soon the grounds will freeze, and we won't be able to dig for clay until spring."

"But I broke her bowl," wondered a puzzled Tessa.

"She will make another," Ayanna assured her.

Tessa was thrilled about the prospect of working with clay. Her first and only attempt at doing so had led to heartbreak. She had made her dog in a ceramics class at the institute when she began attending school there. She had painted him brown and white and kept him on a bookshelf by her bed in her new foster home. After having lost her family, the dog became a kind of surrogate: a pretend pet who kept her company each night as she fell asleep in her unfamiliar surroundings. One day, she came home from school to find that the dog had fallen from the shelf and had broken into several pieces. She too felt broken, and despite her tears, her new foster mother admonished her.

"Who said you could put that thing on one of my bookshelves anyway!" the woman had shrieked.

Tessa was ordered to throw the broken dog away. From then on, she took drawing and painting classes and stayed away from the school's ceramics studio.

Though she wanted so badly to help Nora with her clay, she was anxious about it. She did not want to break any more pieces of pottery and did not want to anger her. She wanted both Nora and Ayanna to like her, so she could remain safely with them until Nora's husband returned with Noah. Besides, they were the sister and mother of Elan, whose company she now missed as well.

# Chapter 10

One week after Tessa disappeared, Matthew Bradbury asked Mr. Gerard and Joshua Peterson if they would meet with him and his wife. When they arrived together at the Bradburys' apartment, Matthew was taken aback by how pale and thin Noah's closest friend had become. As Joshua sat on their couch, telling them the same story he had told Mr. Gerard in the museum, Matthew observed him. Joshua spoke in a soft monotone the entire time, and when he finished speaking, without even waiting for the Bradburys' reaction, he stood up.

"Now that I've told you everything, if you don't mind, I want to go home," Joshua announced.

"Joshua, I want to believe you, I really do," assured Joanne.

"I know, but you don't believe me. I wouldn't believe me either, but I am telling the truth. I'm sorry that I ever agreed to help Tessa."

Joshua then opened the front door to the apartment and walked out. Mr. Gerard remained behind and promised Matthew and Joanne that the story they'd just heard was the same one Joshua had told him at the museum.

"As you know, Rebecca is both Noah's and Joshua's teacher. But Joshua reached out to me and I am going to help support him through all this. Rebecca told me that the boys were close friends and that they have always been levelheaded and responsible kids. Neither of us knows what to make of Joshua's tale," said Mr. Gerard.

"Perhaps Joshua too was hallucinating," Joanne suggested sarcastically.

"It's possible! Hallucinations, along with overactive imaginations, account for a lot of the strange phenomena people report seeing," agreed Mr. Gerard. "But maybe there are still some phenomena we just don't understand."

"As a scientist, I agree there are probably a lot of phenomena we don't understand, or have not yet encountered. I am just not prepared to accept that as an explanation for the disappearance of my kid." Noah's mother spoke softly, in a manner that expressed anger.

"Joanne…" Matthew warned.

"I am sorry. I wish I knew how to be of more help," offered Mr. Gerard. "All I can tell you is that I believe Joshua believes he is telling the truth."

After Mr. Gerard left, Matthew and his wife sat quietly together at the oak table.

"The Joshua I know could never have done anything to harm that girl," said Matthew, breaking their silence.

"Not everyone believes that, Matthew."

"Those who know him best—Mr. Gerard, Ms. Rebecca, and Miguel—all do."

"But how could Joshua sit there and tell us such a story and expect us to believe it?" Joanne mused.

"I agree with Mr. Gerard that Joshua believes he's telling the truth. It's possible he's blocking out what did happen," suggested Matthew.

"That girl was so frail looking, Matthew. I think she shares Noah's love of science fiction. She told me we should continue searching the museum because she believes that—" Joanne stopped speaking in mid-sentence.

"What is it?"

"She believes Noah is still there. So that part of Joshua's story probably is true. Tessa most likely did ask him to accompany her there," noted Joanne.

"Honey, I think I should search the museum once more as well. A colleague of mine who works there offered his office to me. He has a fold-out couch and sometimes spends the night there. He is going to be working at Acadia National Park in Maine for a week."

"Tessa also told me she believed Noah did see the animals come to life. She believed something otherworldly was happening in the museum," Joanne said, without seeming to have heard him.

"Well, I will be writing a letter to the taxidermy department about that one," Matthew quipped.

"You will not!" shouted Joanne.

"I'm kidding," Matthew assured her.

"No, I mean you will not be spending a week at the museum."

"I'll only be there for a couple of days. I will be fine."

"How can you be so sure you'll be fine?" asked Joanne.

"The place is now crawling with detectives and the media. I'll have plenty of company while I'm there."

"I don't think Joshua is telling us everything. What if there are other people involved?" said Joanne.

"The authorities told us they don't believe anyone else was involved. Maybe Tessa's disappearance has nothing to do with Noah's. We now know she was unhappy in her foster home. Maybe Joshua helped her run away and is now protecting her."

"Well if that's true, then he is one very talented liar."

The only thing Matthew Bradbury knew for sure was that the lives of three children were now at stake. A few days after Joshua's visit, he packed his bag and left for the museum. Though closed to the public, scientists and other staff members still had full access to it. When he arrived at its front steps, he found news cameras everywhere. Inside, security professionals were stationed in every hall. Without a word to anyone, Matthew quickly made his way up to his colleague's office.

After spending the afternoon resting on the fold-out couch, Matthew returned to the museum and spent the evening walking through its many galleries. Just before midnight, he walked into the Hall of North American Mammals. The cougar that Joshua said he'd seen come back to life, along with all the other mammals, were as unalive as they'd always been.

Matthew then made his way to the Hall of New York State and the other diorama Joshua had seen return to life. Ignoring the passing security guards who regarded him quizzically, he stationed himself in front of *An October Afternoon Near Stissing Mountain* until sunrise. But that diorama too remained still and lifeless.

The following morning, a bleary-eyed Matthew went to the museum's research library. Though finding his son took precedence, he could not neglect his work. He and his team had to find a way to halt the devastating tree disease as quickly as possible. As he sat thumbing through several botany books, Matthew struggled to concentrate. Perhaps somewhere within one was information that had been overlooked, something that might spark an idea, generate a solution. He was looking at the beautiful color plates of tree leaves in one musty old book when he was suddenly overcome by emotion. Averting his eyes from onlookers, he quickly left the library.

Outside, the day was warm and muggy. Wandering through Central Park, Matthew tried to find a solitary spot where he could sit, dry his tears, and collect himself. He walked along a path, past some frail looking sweet gum and dogwood trees that had been recently planted. There were only a few other people in the park, as overhead a storm system approached. Arriving at an old cast iron bench near a statue of a female astronaut, Matthew sat down and quickly ate the protein wrap he'd brought for lunch.

On his way back to the museum, he stopped by the locked iron gate of a children's playground. The playground was now empty, with all the children presumably safe indoors. As a rumble of approaching thunder sounded, a swirl of wind picked up and blew a spattering of gritty sand in his face.

Matthew thought about how lucky the kids in this neighborhood were. They all went to excellent schools and lived in apartments that were small but clean, safe, climate controlled, and equipped with all the modern conveniences. Looking over the park, Matthew compared it to Joshua's neighborhood and suddenly felt a great admiration for the boy. Matthew could only imagine the kind of obstacles Joshua had to overcome.

Overhead, a cloud looking like a purple fist cast a shadow over the playground. A group of chalk drawings, drawn midway between the sandbox and swings, glowed in the dim light. Pairs of animals—elephants, giraffe, turtles, and lions, all created in vibrant colors—formed a line, walking as if in a parade toward a large structure shaped like a trapezoid. One of the elephants was smiling as it looked at its mate, which made Matthew smile too. He recalled how both his children had drawn similar pictures when they had been four-year-olds.

The trapezoidal structure that the animals were heading toward had an American flag sticking out of its top. Matthew wasn't sure what kind of building it was, though it resembled a long-ago circus tent. When drops of rain started to fall and the drawing began to blur, he decided that it probably depicted the museum rather than a circus tent. It made no difference though. The rain had begun to fall more heavily, and the entire drawing was dissolving into puddles.

Quickly, Matthew slipped his neon-blue rain poncho over his head. Instead of heading back to the museum as he was supposed to, he ran out of the park and across the street to his wife's favorite bookstore. The store's windows were now decorated with little white lights and displays of antique figures for Christmas. Removing and shaking water from his poncho, Matthew stepped through the shop's door as a tiny bell sounded.

The bookstore seemed to have been transported from another century. It was more like a gallery really, one filled with displays of ancient hardcovers and new limited-edition art books. Matthew wandered through its narrow aisles, lined with rickety wooden bookcases, searching for what—he did not know. Slowly, he meandered through the fiction and nonfiction sections. As he passed by shelves of young-adult books, the cover illustration of one caught his eye and he turned back.

There, sitting on top of a bookcase, waiting to be put back into its proper place, was a copy of *A Wrinkle in Time.*

Matthew picked the book up and felt the weight of it in his hands. Opening its cover, he saw it had been printed the same year as the copy Noah owned. There were several stains on its pages, most likely from water and food. Noah's book, he noted, was in much better condition. A rogue tear escaped from Matthew's eye and fell onto the book's title page. "I'll have to buy it if I'm not careful," he thought. Turning the book over, he looked at its price tag. It was worth a good chunk of money. After putting it back on the shelf, he looked for his own childhood favorite, *The Chronicles of Narnia: The Lion, The Witch, and The Wardrobe.* Had Joshua read this book? Had this book given Joshua the idea for the story he'd told them?

Matthew was about to leave the store when a torrential rain began to fall. Outside, the wild wind tossed a willow tree to and fro, while rivulets of water formed along the street. As he waited among a group of people for the deluge to subside, he realized something. The animals in the children's park were not walking into a circus tent or the museum. They were walking onto Noah's ark.

# Chapter 11

At the institute, all students were required to learn how to swim. Noah was a fairly decent swimmer, but in recent years he preferred running track. It wasn't that he didn't like to swim. The problem was that the only place to do so was at the institute's indoor pool, which was always crowded and way too warm. While there, Noah's claustrophobia often kicked in. He always thought that if the flesh-eating microbe had not infested the lake near his grandparents' home upstate, he would have loved swimming there. But now here he was, being given an opportunity to swim in just such a lake, and he was unable to enter its water. The lake, though pristine, was just too cold.

"You went swimming in the mountain stream. This is the same water," Taman called from a rocky ledge.

"The stream was much warmer and not as deep as this lake," Noah called back, wondering how Taman had found out about that.

Wanting Taman to approve of him, Noah forced himself to wade into the frigid water up to his knees. As he stood there, a painful, tingling sensation spread through the nerve endings in his lower legs. He was about to rebel and walk out of the lake when Taman stood up on the ledge and, in one quick motion, dove into the water. Noah watched, feeling the weight of his own weakness.

Entering the lake all at once looked to be easier than walking into it one step at a time. Leaving the lake, Noah walked up to the ledge Taman had dove from and looked down at the water. In the depths below, he saw the shadows of large rocks. He would need to clear them and land in the deeper water a few feet away. This would be easier to do if he were an experienced diver. But Noah was not a diver, and instead he would have to jump in feet first. Though afraid, Noah grit his teeth, held his breath, and kicked away from the rock as far as he could.

The fall was fast, and only after the water stopped his trajectory did he register its temperature. His chest constricted and his ears and head ached as he scrambled to the surface. Once there, he gasped for air and forced himself to keep moving. His body shook as he swam in a dog paddle to the center of the lake and back. When he returned to the beach, he looked up to see Taman nodding his head in approval. Coughing and spitting, his skin a bluish color, Noah wrapped his fur cloak around his shoulders and huddled close to the warm fire.

For the next several days, Noah walked into the lake instead of jumping into it from the ledge. He grew accustomed, or rather resigned, to the frigid early morning swims. His body recalled what it had been taught years ago, and he stopped dog paddling and began swimming the crawl stroke. With his face in the water, he propelled his arms one over the other while kicking his legs. On every fourth stroke, he turned his head to the side to breathe. He even remembered to flatten his hands and pull the water behind him and to turn them sideways after each stroke, so they would not drag on his glide forward.

One morning, he emerged from the lake to find that Taman had extinguished their fire. Knowing that its warmth awaited him every morning was in part what enabled him to endure swimming. Each time he emerged from the lake, he couldn't wait to sit by the fire and thaw out while drinking hot tea. Now the fire was gone and even though he was wrapped up in his fur, he still shivered. He looked at Taman disdainfully, but the man said nothing.

Lighting a fire was one of the tasks Noah was expected to master. In his world, fires were lit mainly for aesthetic purposes, to create a kind of atmosphere. To do so, one simply passed a hand over a device that generated a flame. In Taman's world, knowing how to light a fire was essential for survival. Since arriving in the mountains, Noah had tried to create one by hitting together the piece of flint and the steel knife he'd found in his pack. He'd managed to generate sparks, but they refused to ignite the nest of grass beneath them.

Without waiting for his numb fingers to regain their full flexibility, Noah set upon the task expected of him. He formed a new nest from the dried grass that had already been collected. Again, he hit the steel knife against the flintstone and blew the generated sparks onto the grassy bed. After an hour of hard work, after his hands and neck glands ached from overuse, one speck miraculously separated from its cluster and floated delicately down onto the tip of a blade of grass.

Despite the pain in his neck glands, with a breath weighed and measured, Noah blew on this one individual spark. It began to glow brightly, and Noah watched as the determined speck ate up the grass and traveled into the heart of the nest. When a small flame leapt up from the papery bed, Noah leapt up as well. He quickly tossed small twigs onto the burning nest, and when they too caught fire he added larger sticks and branches. As a full blaze burst forth, Noah stood up, raised his arms to the sky, and let out a whooping yell of joy.

"The spirit of the crow watches over you," Taman noted dryly.

Noah felt slightly ashamed by his unabashed and sporty show of emotion. Still, it was an exhilarating moment, one he would never forget.

A few days later, on a chilly morning, he and Taman set off from their camp to one of the farther mountains in the range. On their way, they marked a trail with stacks of rocks and broken twigs to help them find their way back. When they reached the mountain, they climbed to its summit and looked out over the landscape of endless trees. In the distance, Taman pointed to a thin, silvery thread winding its way snakelike across the land.

"You must make your way to The River That Flows Two Ways. You need to befriend it and follow its course. It will bring you to the great island where the tree is believed to reside," Taman told him.

Noah squinted at the distant river, known in his own time as the Hudson River. He felt a sinking feeling in his stomach. How could anyone possibly walk that far? There were so many things to remember and so many mistakes to be made. To succeed on this journey, Noah would have to rely on his own instincts and become his own disciplinarian. He would have to maintain vigilant control over his daydreamy nature.

Taman pointed overhead, where two large birds were soaring against the pale purple clouds.

"The great hawks are looking for prey," he told Noah.

Most likely a mating couple, the hawks repeatedly separated and returned to one another. Noah looked up at them and felt envious. It would take the birds no time at all to fly to the river. He felt the same respect for them that he did for anyone who could do something he wished he could do.

As he took in a deep breath, he noticed that a smell of smoke had filled the air. Taman led him to the other side of the mountain's summit, in the direction from which the smoke came. There, a dark cloud hovered over a burning forest fire below. Taman explained that the fire had been set to clear away dead trees, fallen leaves, and other debris. Setting the fire in a contained area prevented a more dangerous and uncontrollable one from occurring. In the spring, there would be room for new plants to grow. The tender green shoots would attract and foster the population of deer and other animals.

Noah thought about all the animals he had seen back in the American Museum of Natural History. He thought about the whale, cougar, and wolf, who had led him into this world, believing that he had it in him to find the Great Oak. Noah now understood that all these creatures were his equals, and that they deserved to be treated that way.

"Everyone here hunts animals. In my world, our government protects all our animals, and it's a crime to hurt or kill them," said Noah brazenly.

"We depend on many of our animals for survival. We live closely with them, respect them, and know that this planet belongs to us all," Taman replied. "But many of our new neighbors don't share our views and for centuries, their views will prevail. People will exclude animals, take away their homes, and endanger their futures. By the time your era arrives, many animals will no longer exist. In your world, the balance of life is broken and needs mending. That is why you are here."

They walked down the mountain in silence. Noah felt stung by Taman's words, mostly because he knew that Taman was right. It was not appropriate for Noah to hold Taman's world to the moral standards of his own. This was the way it was here, and as with the mystery that was life itself, Noah had to accept it and be thankful for the food he ate and the clothing he now wore.

The day after their hike to the mountain, Taman caught the deer he'd been hoping for. While the deer was being butchered, Noah set off in search of chestnuts, firewood, and anything else he could think of. When he returned, he found meat smoking on the fire and skins drying on the ground. No part of the animal would be wasted. Though Noah felt uncomfortable about hunting, he knew that the deer's meat and skins were enabling him to survive in Taman's world.

The past few nights had become much colder, and in the mornings a white frost blanketed the ground. That evening as they ate roasted deer meat, along with the chestnuts and wild onions Noah had found, Taman told him that it was time for him to embark on his journey. Taman explained that it would grow colder yet, and that snow would soon cover the ground making traveling difficult.

"I don't know if I can to do this," Noah said quietly.

"You found the mountain stream, swam in the lake, and lit the morning fire. You are one who does not give up. I have faith in you."

"Taman, I am sorry for what I said about hunting. Sometimes I say ridiculous things."

Taman nodded. "If you don't object to fishing, tomorrow we will catch river trout and prepare a meal to celebrate the end of your training."

"What happens if I am not able to find this tree?" asked Noah.

"We must believe that you will." Taman smiled sadly.

Noah felt his heart sinking. He knew that soon he would be separating from the company of his friend and the security he provided. Taman would return to his family as Noah set off on his lonely expedition to find the oak tree.

People enter and leave our lives all the time. Some leave an indelible imprint on our being that changes and shapes us. Though they were together only a brief time, Taman had this impact on Noah. He would help determine the kind of man Noah would become.

On the morning of their final day together, Taman fished for trout in the lake while Noah, who was unable to do so himself, listened to him tell stories about the new settlers who were arriving from Europe. He spoke of their farms, their new ways, and the supplies they brought to the region. He told Noah more about the fur trading industry with which most were involved and about the tensions it brought to the people who lived in the river valley.

"Always remember why you are here," warned Taman. "Do not reveal your identity or mission to anyone who does not address you first by your name."

Taman caught three river trout. After cleaning them, he coated each one with wet clay that was found nearby. When the fire was hot enough, the clay-covered trout were placed within its circle of heat and covered with burning twigs. Wild onions, roots, and chestnuts were added to roast as well. When the clay had hardened and turned white hot, Taman removed it from the fire. After it cooled somewhat, he cracked it open with a rock to reveal the steaming, flaky white meat inside. The meal of baked fish and vegetables was perhaps the best meal Noah had ever eaten. Still, it was permeated with loss.

Noah had traveled back in time, four hundred and fifty years. Couldn't he stop time for another day or two, so he could remain here a little longer? Focusing intently on extracting meat from chestnuts, he hardly noticed the soreness in his fingernails. Somewhere in the distance, a wolf howled a deep and mournful song that seemed to express the emotions Noah felt within his own heart. Despite his sadness, Noah knew he had to remain strong.

# Chapter 12

On a sunny morning as crisp as a new fall apple, Tessa set off with Ayanna and her mother to the ceramics worksite. Nora had decided to bring the girls to the worksite to help her finish the pottery she'd made a few weeks earlier. She hoped to get her work ready for an upcoming market, the final one of the fall season.

Tessa and Ayanna walked behind Nora who led the family's horse, the same one that had carried Tessa to the village on the night she'd arrived. Once again, the horse carried supplies: blankets, extra clothes, and enough smoked meat, flatbread, and cornmeal to last them for the duration of their stay. As they walked through the herb-scented woods, the horse happily swished her tail while Tessa filled the pocket of her dress with autumn treasures—colorful leaves and seeds to add to her collection.

Tessa had no problem keeping up with Ayanna. She had no shortness of breath, and the feeling that her legs would buckle and give way beneath her was nonexistent. She took wide strides, stretching her leg muscles as she planted each foot solidly on the ground. Though she had no idea where her strength was coming from, Tessa was immensely grateful for it.

At midmorning, they arrived at the ceramics camp. It was situated in a clearing in the woods and consisted primarily of three wooden huts. One of the huts contained sleeping mats and was used as a shelter. The other two were used for storage, one for ceramics, and the other for food and general supplies.

Several families shared this worksite, and they all contributed to its upkeep. Tessa spotted a now darkened firepit, whose center was lined with flat stones. Beneath some hickory trees, there were two long tables. One table bore a spread of several different tools made from bone, broken pieces of pottery, and fire-hardened wood. The other table was covered by a pale-yellow stone slab.

Nora spread some of the food she had brought with them on the table with the yellow stone slab. After she and the girls ate lunch, they began setting up their camp. While Ayanna swept in and around the shelter hut, Tessa helped Nora rummage through the supply shed for the things they needed. They took out some dried herbs, maple syrup, and two pails for carrying water. Tessa found an old birchbark box that Nora had once used for storing bread. It was so dirty now that Nora allowed her to keep it for her seed collection.

While Nora worked on lighting a fire, Tessa and Ayanna carried the two pails to a nearby lake to fill them with water. They hiked to the top of a small hill where they stopped and looked out at the landscape. Though it was not easy for Tessa to see into the distance, she could see enough of the scene before her to know it was a beautiful one. Golden light, cast by the afternoon sun, emblazoned the sea of yellow-leafed trees and shimmered across the flat surface of the lake. Overhead, a flock of birds formed the letter V. They moved like a single animal, pulsing beneath the white clouds that floated across the blue sky. Tessa wished she had her computer's camera or better still her paint set, so she could capture this view and bring it back with her when she returned to her world.

"Those birds are preparing for their journey," said Ayanna looking up at the sky. "Soon winter will be upon us. Come, we must be going. There is much to do before this day is over."

Grabbing onto shrubs with her free hand, being careful not to slip on dirt or rocks that moved underfoot, Tessa slowly followed Ayanna down the hill's steep slope. After filling their pails with water at the lake, something they would do many times during their stay, they headed back to their camp by a longer, though easier, route, around the hill instead of back over it.

That evening, after a meal of corn cakes with maple syrup, they sat and rested by the fire while the sun set. Ayanna and her mother worked on their sewing projects, Ayanna on a leather purse and her mother on a shawl, while Tessa, who was just learning to sew, practiced on the scrap materials Nora had given her. The night air became quite chilly, and though they were all tired, it was Nora who first retreated into the hut. Neither Tessa nor Ayanna were ready to let go of the day, and so they remained sitting by the fire.

"There are signs this winter will be a cold and stormy one," said Ayanna without looking up from her work. "The wooly caterpillar's fur has grown thick, and some animals, bears and rabbits, have become very fat."

"Where I come from, summer is our hardest season. It gets so hot and muggy that it's hard to breathe, and you can get very sick. We spend a lot of time in cooling shelters. Winter is cooler than summer, although it is never as cold as it is here," said Tessa, as she wrapped the shawl Nora had given her around her shoulders.

"This is not cold!" said Ayanna, looking up from her sewing.

"Well it certainly feels cold to me," replied Tessa.

"Come winter, the lake and the streams will freeze, and a deep snow will cover the Earth," Ayanna informed her.

"I've read about the long-ago winters. I am sure I will have gone back to my own world by the time it snows," Tessa affirmed, though her expression was one of worry.

Ayanna suggested that they set up their sleeping mats outside so as not to disturb her mother, who was most likely sound asleep in the hut. Tessa curled up in a blanket and lay on a mat near the banked fire. She gazed up at the moon and thought about the people back in her own time who might be upset that she too was now missing: her doctor and social worker, her teacher Mr. Gerard, and probably Noah's mother, now that Tessa had met her. Joshua, of course, would be upset.

"Joshua!" Tessa sat up, horrified.

"What is it?" asked Ayanna.

"I left my best friend behind in the museum. I asked him to help me find Noah... and now? I just know I got him into trouble."

"If he helped you enter our world for a noble cause, then he too will have great spirits protecting him."

Tessa felt comforted by this. She lay back down, turned to face the fire, and watched its untamable sparks snapping and flying in every direction. While waiting for sleep, it occurred to her how ironic it was that she had traveled back in time. For the past two years, she had been fantasizing about returning to an earlier period in her life to be with her family again. If only she hadn't traveled back so far. As she drifted into sleep, Tessa envisioned her world—its heat and crowds, its dirty water and droughts—and wondered how it had ever evolved from this world of New Netherland.

The following morning, Nora woke the girls early. They were to spend much of the day excavating clay from what was now a dry riverbed. Long ago, the river had been full of rushing water and mating trout all struggling to make their way back to the lake. Now it was known for rich clay deposits that were exceptionally good for pottery making. The ceramics worksite had been built to offer proximity to the old river.

Nora and the two girls each carried their own bucket and tools as they hiked through the woods. When they arrived at the dry bed, they immediately began digging up clay. Tessa scooped up a mound of the reddish-brown mud and feeling its weight and texture, wondered at the miracle of such a substance being transformed into a mug or bowl. She was removing twigs and rocks when she noticed one stone shaped like a teardrop. It was flat and smooth with a tip that came to a point. Nora examined it and then spoke excitedly in words Tessa did not understand. Ayanna told her that she had found an arrowhead and that it looked to be a very old one. Such a find was sure to bring them great luck.

For the next two days, they made several trips to the riverbed, returning to the worksite after each one with heavy buckets full of clay. Some of this clay would be cleaned and prepared for immediate use, but most of it would be stored in a covered hole that had been dug into the ground behind the storage sheds.

To clean the clay, Nora diluted it with water in a large bucket, stirring it until it became a soupy mess. She then removed pebbles and sticks, before straining it through a woven cloth to remove smaller pieces of debris. Afterward, she spread the watery slop onto the table that was covered by the flat stone. Ayanna told Tessa that her father had obtained the stone through trade with settlers who used it to construct new buildings. Known as limestone, it absorbed water and made the clay dry more quickly.

Overnight, the limestone did its job and in the morning Nora scraped the clay off the table and formed it into two small mounds. Tessa and Ayanna were each given a mound along with a portion of clay from the supply that had been previously cleaned and stored. Now they each had enough clay to make their own pots.

They began by kneading their clay to soften it and remove air pockets that could make a pot explode when it was fired. While pounding and pushing with the palms of their hands, they added a small amount of sand to their clay to make it stronger. Tessa worked so hard at this that her back and shoulders ached. Clay and sand became painfully caked beneath her fingernails and when Nora told them they could stop kneading, Tessa was greatly relieved.

Ayanna, who had been helping her mother with ceramics for a while, patiently waited while Nora demonstrated her pottery-making technique for Tessa. Working at the limestone table, Nora flattened a small ball of clay into a circular disk. Then, rolling another ball of clay between her palms, she formed a long coil that she pressed around the disk's edge. More coils were stacked on top of the first one until a cylinder was formed. When it was tall enough, Nora used a flat tool, shaped like the arrowhead Tessa had found, to blend the coils and smooth the sides of what looked to be a vase.

By repeating each of the steps Nora had shown her, Tessa built her own tube-shaped jar. Deciding that her jar needed a lid, she asked Ayanna, who only wanted to make a small bowl, if she could have her extra clay. Ayanna agreed and Tessa, after making her lid, had clay left over. Though she was wary about doing so, she decided to use the extra clay to recreate the dog she had made at the institute. Using her share of the arrowhead's good luck, she made a wish that her new dog would be protected from ever breaking.

Over the next two days, the two girls helped Nora prepare the pottery she had previously made for firing. The girls helped to sand down the pots' sides and then watched as Nora, using a sharpened piece of a deer's antler, carved designs—leaves, waves, and graceful cattails—into them. After the sides of each pot were burnished with a smooth stone, they were ready for painting. Tessa was thrilled to learn that she and Ayanna would apply the paint, using brushes made from animal hair. They coated the pots with a watered-down clay, to which crushed charcoal, herbs, and berries had been added.

When the pottery was ready for firing, the girls helped gather branches for the roaring blaze that Nora built in the fire-pit. Only a few bowls and mugs were fired at a time. They were placed near, but not directly within, the fire's center. When the pieces of pottery became accustomed to the heat, Nora covered them with burning branches and grass. They baked for almost two hours, before Nora knocked them away from the fire with a stick. Tessa thought the charred-looking pieces were ruined. But after they cooled and were cleaned, they were beautiful.

It took several days to fire all of Nora's pottery. During the last few batches, there was enough room in the firepit for Tessa's lidded jar and dog, and Ayanna's small bowl. The late October air had become quite chilly, and the two girls sat close to the fire's heat, sipping mugs of tea while their pots baked. When her clay pieces were finished, Tessa was dismayed to find a small crack in the side of her jar.

"My mother always puts a mistake in her pots. Perfection attracts jealousy and bad luck," Ayanna told her.

Nora's approach gave Tessa permission to feel proud of her dog and lidded jar, despite their imperfections. Tessa had always sought to make everything perfect or close to it, and not having to do so would be such a relief. She decided that when she returned home, she would continue taking ceramics classes at the institute and not worry how anyone felt about her work. One day, she might even make pottery as beautiful as Nora's.

Despite the chilly nights, Ayanna and Tessa continued to sleep outside by the fire while Nora slept in the hut. One night as Tessa slept, she was woken up by the sound of loud singing. When she opened her eyes, she saw Ayanna hastily throwing dirt over the fire and knew that something must be wrong. Ayanna put a finger to her mouth and motioned for her to follow silently. Quickly, Tessa got up and, by the light of the moon, followed Ayanna who led the horse to an area behind the campsite.

"We must warn your mother," whispered Tessa.

"She will be fine," Ayanna assured her.

The two girls remained still, listening to the fearful sounds of raucous singing and drunken laughter. Suddenly, the men's voices ceased and from somewhere nearby, Tessa heard the sound of a low, rumbling voice. This new presence seemed to frighten the horse even more than the men had, and Ayanna had to hold tightly onto her.

Tessa now understood that this world, like her own, had its share of badly behaved people. The two girls returned to the hut where they found Nora awake and holding her cooking knife by her side. She looked at them both solemnly, before speaking sternly to her daughter.

"We are to sleep inside for the rest of our stay," Ayanna told Tessa.

The two girls brought their sleeping mats into the little house. It was crowded, but they each managed to find their own space on the dirt floor. As Tessa lay on her mat, she listened for further sounds of the cougar. She wondered why the big cat had returned. Had she come to protect Tessa, or bring her back to her own time? Tessa didn't know whether Ayanna and Nora were aware of the presence of her fearsome friend.

While Ayanna and her mother slept, Tessa got up and stepped outside. Carefully, she made her way in the moonlight to the horse who was now calm and still. Standing close to the horse's warm body, Tessa scanned the perimeter of the worksite. Through the trees, she spotted two vibrant yellow dots glowing like miniature versions of the orb overhead.

"I'm here," she called softly.

The eyes stared briefly into her own, before the form to which they were attached vanished into the shadows. Tessa waited for several minutes before returning to the hut.

The following night, Nora's decision that the girls remain in the small house proved to be a good one. In the middle of the night, the strong odor of a skunk permeated the air, and early in the morning, a bear was heard rummaging for the food he would need to further fatten himself up for the cold winter ahead. Nora interpreted the encounter as a sign that it was time to return to the village.

After cleaning the worksite, they repacked the now finished pottery back into the ceramics shed. Nora would ask Elan and another young man to bring it back to the village in the family wagon. As they began their journey back to the village, Tessa, who had been permitted to bring her clay dog with her, walked while holding it tightly to her chest.

# Chapter 13

The morning Noah set off on his journey, Taman assured him that part of his spirit would travel with him. But once Noah was alone and heading deeper into the woods, the only way Taman felt present was by way of the things Noah carried. Everything Noah had with him had been given to him by Taman: his steel knife and flintstone, his deerskin clothing and pack, and the mantle made of raccoon fur. The mantle, which was presently unneeded and draped over Noah's pack, had once belonged to Taman's son. He was about Noah's age, and Noah couldn't help but wonder if they would have been friends had they met.

The trail Noah took was the one Taman had walked him to, the one that would lead him all the way to the river. It was an old rustic trail that seemed seldom used. At times, it faded from view, blending into the floor of the forest, and sometimes it disappeared altogether beneath piles of fall leaves. Each time the trail vanished, Noah anxiously continued to follow its assumed course, until with immense relief he regained sight of it once more.

Overhead, clouds had begun to move in, casting purple shadows throughout the woods. As the museum had, the woods now felt ominous, haunted and filled with the unknown. It occurred to Noah that at some point in the future, this late autumn season would become the time of Halloween. He recalled the frightening old stories he'd been told as a child, of long-ago forests filled with witches, zombies, and other monsters. Back then he'd been thankful that there were hardly any forests left in his world. Now, here he was traveling through one on a mission to bring them back to his own time.

The surrounding woods were eerily quiet and still, with a smell of smoke faintly permeating the chilly air. By now the trees had dropped most of their leaves. In the newly open spaces, Noah could see into the surrounding distance, and as he hiked, his overactive imagination began to plague him once more. He was hurrying along, when up ahead he spotted a gnarled and hunched-over figure standing on the side of the trail. As he got closer, though, the frightening apparition turned out to be no more than a tree, with crooked branches and a trunk covered in burls.

"I'm sorry!" Noah yelled out, for having failed to recognize the tree. He knew from his father that burls meant the tree was sick.

Noah tried to view the forest for what it was. A place filled with living beings who needed protection. Though his fear somewhat subsided, he still felt the weight of aloneness, and he began to comfort himself by conjuring up the companionship of family and friends.

"What a magnificent place this is. Thank you for bringing me here. How did you ever find it?" Noah imagined his father talking to him as they walked side by side.

"I think it found me," answered Noah.

"If you want to know the truth, my neighborhood is much scarier than this place. Still, if there is any need to run, I will let you know in plenty of time," Joshua might say if he were here.

"Thanks, Josh!" said Noah.

Noah was engaging with his imaginary guests when he was stopped once more, this time by the sound of branches snapping behind him. Turning around, he saw two foraging deer standing on the trail. A large male with twitching ears held his head high, while his female companion stood timidly behind him. Perhaps they had heard Noah talking to himself and sought to investigate. They remained only briefly, before the female abruptly turned and ran back into the woods. The male quickly bolted after her, and Noah, who noted his sharp-pointed antlers, was not sorry.

"Go in peace and safety," he whispered, thinking about the clothing he wore and the meat he ate.

Just as his heart rate returned to normal, from somewhere in the sea of trees there was a burst of loud, rowdy shouts. The voices were followed by a cracking sound and then a crash of something huge falling to the earth. Noah remembered Taman telling him how the Great Oak was now in danger of being cut down for her wood. Though he could not see the loggers, he could hear them, and even though he objected to what they were doing, Noah felt grateful for their human presence.

As the sun began to set, Noah began to search for a place to camp. He was scanning the area when a familiar caw sounded in the woods off the trail. Perched on the uppermost branch of a hickory tree, Noah spotted the crow. He felt sure that it was the bird from the museum and that it was following him and noting his progress. Remembering that Taman had said crows bring good luck, Noah stepped off the trail and walked over to the hickory tree. It stood among a small cluster of trees, in whose center was a bare patch of ground. There, Noah dropped his pack and began to set up his camp.

Though Noah knew that by lighting a fire after sunset he could attract unwanted attention, he decided to do so anyway. The woods were becoming colder and less hospitable now that darkness was falling. Now an experienced fire starter, he gathered whatever dry twigs and grass he could find and managed to ignite a flame before all the sun's light had disappeared. After securely banking the fire with rocky soil, he wrapped the raccoon fur around himself and lay down. The snapping flames brought warmth, light, and a sense of security, all of which allowed Noah to sleep.

The next morning was a raw and dreary one. Setting off early, Noah walked while eating his first meal of the day, a ration of the smoked deer meat and flatbread that Taman had prepared for him. When it began to rain heavily, Noah pushed himself to maintain his walking pace over the muddied trail. It rained up until midday, just as he arrived at a spot where a new, well-worn trail intersected with his own. Looking through the western line of now leafless woods, he yelled out with joy. There, shimmering beneath the clearing sky, was the majestic river.

When Noah reached the river, he walked out onto a landmass that jutted into the water. There, he sat down on a small beach that ran along its southern side and looked up at the river that moved toward New Amsterdam. Overhead, the cloud cover was breaking up, and wisps of white gauze moved across the sky. As the sun broke through, its light fractured the river's surface into broad swatches of silvery white, pale blue, and a deep slate blue. Along the shoreline, trees dressed in the last remnants of autumn—red, gold, and deep green—cast their colors out onto the water.

As Noah sat listening to the rhythmic sound of pebbles being pulled back and forth by small waves rolling onto the beach, he caught a movement out of the corner of his eye. He looked to the right in time to see the bow of a boat gliding into view from behind the trees at the tip of the landmass. Quickly, he ducked behind a nearby log and lay down flat on his stomach.

The long slender canoe bore three men and passed by in full view of the beach. The two men sitting in front wore black capes, while a third in the back wore a fur cloak. The men in front looked straight ahead as they paddled, but the man in back, who had two lines painted on the left side of his face, turned and looked in Noah's direction. When the boat had traveled far enough away so that its size was reduced to that of a child's toy, Noah emerged from hiding. Though he'd planned to, he would not be able to walk beside the river.

Retracing his steps, he walked back to the well-worn trail which ran parallel to the river. This road was probably one used by the new settlers, and though Noah knew he should stay clear of it and the settlements, he was now in need of water. He'd been afraid to draw water from the river. Taman had warned him that even in this world, water in areas of human activity had become unsafe to drink. Noah hoped the road would lead him to a farm, where there would be a fresh water source nearby.

Late in the afternoon, the possibility of finding water appeared in the form of two girls, who wore long woolen capes and white bonnets over their hair. The girls, who each carried a bucket, were so engaged in conversation that they barely noticed Noah as they walked by him. When they left the road and began trotting over the brown grass of an open field, Noah followed them. They stopped at a small wooden structure and dipped their buckets into its center, while Noah ran to the edge of the field, lay down by the trees, and waited.

The girls seemed to take forever to fill their buckets with water. When they finally did, they walked away, spilling drops of the precious liquid onto the ground. Feeling like the small animal that he was, Noah watched them anxiously until they disappeared along the road that he supposed would bring them home. Only then did he run up to the well and drink as much water as his stomach could hold. After filling his flask one last time, he hurried away.

The sun was now descending into the western edge of the sky, and Noah quickly turned his attention to his next pressing need, that of finding a place to camp for the night. With the possibility of more rain, he knew he would either have to find or construct a shelter. There was no time to build the kind of dwelling he and Taman had made. Instead, he searched for a small tree or bush that would offer protection. About a half mile from the well, he found what he was looking for.

Beneath a tangled and mixed group of shrubs and young trees, Noah found a space large enough to lie down in. Pushing through a dense mass of spiky branches, he began clearing the ground of rocks and sticks while searching for bugs. Back in the mountains, he had seen all kinds of crawling creatures: spiders whose webs looked like glittering galaxies, beetles armed with clawlike pincers, and even a pretty patterned snake that Taman assured him was harmless. With the arrival of morning frosts, they all seemed to disappear. In his world, disease-carrying insects were always present, and one had to be constantly on the lookout for them.

The days were becoming shorter in this world of no electricity and once the sun had set, the nights were now darker and colder than anything Noah had ever experienced before. Unable to light a fire, he wrapped his fur around himself as he settled into the crawl space beneath the dry and brittle branches. Breathing in the tangy mixture of fall leaves and pine needles, he quickly fell asleep. When a steady November rain began to fall in the middle of the night, he woke briefly to discover that the ground around him remained dry.

Noah fell asleep once more and did not wake up again until just before sunrise. Peering through his shelter's branches, he was happy to see the rain had stopped. He was about to retreat into his shelter and close his eyes once more when a little red fox stepped into view. The fox, glowing in the pre-dawn twilight, looked directly toward Noah, as if he knew Noah was hidden in the bushes. Remembering the fox in the diorama, Noah wondered if this animal too might be checking up on him. Suddenly, from somewhere nearby, a dog barked and the fox darted back into the woods.

The dog's bark was followed by the sound of men's voices. Noah quickly packed his things, crawled out from the shrubs, and looked around. The eastern edge of the sky was now a mauve color, while overhead the last few stars and planets blinked on the rising curtain of night. It would be dark and treacherous to do so, but Noah's instincts told him it would be better to hike through the woods than on the trail by which he'd arrived.

The floor of the woods was uneven and littered with sticks and rocks hidden beneath rain-soaked leaves. As the sun rose, Noah quickened his pace, recalling Taman's warning about the dangerous areas in the river valley. He was trying put distance between himself and what now sounded like a group of men and dogs, when he carelessly stepped into a hole and turned his left ankle. Falling face down into the slippery mess, the wet leaves muffled his cry.

Tears of anger fell down Noah's cheeks as he examined his ankle. He would have to take a risk and ask what was most likely a group of hunters for help. While awaiting their arrival, the black crow returned and flew onto the tree above him.

"Have you come to bring me more good luck?" Noah softly hissed.

The bird looked down at Noah. Something about this exchange let Noah know with certainty that rather than ask the hunters for help, he must hide from them. Unable to stand, he buried himself in leaves and lay still as the group passed. Only when it was safe did he crawl out from hiding. Was it possible that the hunters were searching not for animals but for a person? Noah wondered if he had been seen trespassing at the settlement's well.

While looking all around for the crow, who was now nowhere to be seen, Noah spotted a large branch that he thought might make a good crutch. Crawling over to it, he stripped it of its smaller offshoots. The branch was a strong and sturdy one, and Noah realized he was lucky to have found it. Now that he had something to lean on, he could walk more easily, though he could no longer do so over the wood's rough terrain. He had no choice but to return to the smoother surface of the trail.

At midday, Noah sat down to elevate and rest his ankle over a fallen log. Like the log, his ankle felt wooden and stiff, and though he knew he should eat some of Taman's smoked deer meat, he had no appetite. All around him the woods were suspiciously quiet. A cold wind shook the trees, tossing the last of their burnt-looking leaves to the ground. Withdrawing into himself, Noah was so dejected that he didn't even notice the boy who approached him.

Skinny and hungry-looking, the boy, who appeared to be about Noah's age, walked up to Noah and dropped a stack of beaver skin pelts on the ground. He pointed to Noah's raccoon wrap and, using hand gestures, indicated that he wanted to make a trade. Noah had no desire to part with the fur Taman had given him. He depended on it for warmth and survival and he shook his head no. But the agitated boy refused to accept this as an answer. Taking a knife from his pants, he bent down and demanded it.

Joshua and Miguel had once debated over what to do in just this sort of situation. Miguel had argued that it was best to start talking and keep talking.

"Chat him up and up," he had declared.

But Miguel lived at the protected institute, and Joshua, who lived in the real world, had disagreed.

"I am not chatting anybody up," Joshua had said. "I am walking away if I can, running if I have to, and handing over whatever I have if need be."

Noah was unable to walk, let alone run, and chatting someone up who was using hand gestures to communicate seemed rather pointless. Noah took off his wrap and handed it over to the boy. The thief then emptied Noah's pack, taking his knife, flintstone, water pouch, and the remainder of his food. He packed it all into what looked like a burlap bag and then quickly fled into the woods. At least the boy thief had the decency to leave Noah with his pack and the stack of beaver skins. Though unwanted, the furs were a payment of sorts.

The motivating sound of barking dogs prompted Noah to get up and leave the area as well. Stuffing the beaver skins into his now empty pack, he began limping away from the sound of the dogs, toward the river. The boy, he noted, had run away from the dogs as well, though he had headed inland. With his now heavy pack strapped to his back and his need to rely on the stick for support, Noah moved slowly.

When he arrived at the river, the sound of hunters approached once more, this time from the opposite direction. Crawling behind a cluster of dry weeds, cattails, and red sumac, he watched as the group of men and dogs assembled about a hundred yards from where he hid. Someone must have done something terrible, he thought, as he watched them confer with one another.

Remaining hidden, Noah peered through the shrubs and watched as the group split in two. Some continued their search further along the river, while others remained, slowly and intently examining the area. One of the men walked toward him with his hound. They came so close that Noah could see there was a button missing from the man's coat. When the man turned away, despite every instinct he had, Noah crawled to the river and, holding his breath, slid into the water. Anchoring himself between rocks, it took all his strength not to cry out. The river's cold water made the lake water seem tepid.

The hound sniffed and whined, drawing the man's attention once more to the area where Noah had been hiding. Ducking underwater, Noah raised only his mouth above its surface. How he wished the man and his dog would leave. His forehead and eyes throbbed with pain and his ears felt as if they would explode. Still, he had no choice but to remain in the water. Soon though, all sensation of pain was replaced by a feeling of numbness and an overwhelming urge to fall asleep.

# Chapter 14

When Joanne Bradbury's husband, Matthew, called to tell her that he was extending his stay at the museum, she vehemently objected. The holidays were less than a week away, and their daughter Madeleine's school vacation was about to begin. But then her husband asked that she join him there. Reluctantly, she agreed, under the condition that they stay for just one night. Joanne did not want to be apart from Madeleine any longer.

When she arrived at the museum, Joanne found Matthew sitting on its steps reading a book. She called out to him and he looked up and smiled sadly. Together, they walked into Central Park to Matthew's favorite bench, where they sat down and quietly ate the lunch she had brought.

"I spoke to Tessa's foster mother," Joanne informed her husband, interrupting their silence. "All she did was complain to me about her. She is more upset about Tessa stealing her money card than she is about her being missing."

In her mind, Joanne saw Tessa seated before her, large brown eyes peering out through oversized glasses. Matthew didn't say anything. He just continued to stare at the park beyond.

"I also found out that at the very least, Joshua will be accused as a minor of trespassing." Joanne looked intently at her husband, waiting for his reaction, but he remained silent. "Mr. Gerard asked me if I could speak to someone at the school about reinstating Joshua. Apparently, he and many other teachers feel that Joshua's expulsion was unjust. I'm not sure I can do that. It's not that I believe he is guilty. I just don't know what to think."

"I believe Joshua is innocent," her husband replied firmly.

"What makes you think that?"

"I found a copy of Noah's book in that fancy bookstore you love. You should see what they are asking for it," he replied.

"What does that have to do with anything?" Joanne asked with irritation.

"I also found a copy of my favorite childhood book. Do you remember what that was?"

"Yes, I remember. But what does that have to do with Joshua?" Joanne sounded annoyed.

"I am not sure yet, but I believe Joshua has been telling the truth."

"I'm sure there are aspects of his story that are true," Joanne conceded. "I already told you that I believe Tessa did ask him to sneak into the museum with her. In one of my favorite young adult books, a girl convinces her younger brother to run away and hide out in the Metropolitan Museum of Art. She doesn't, however, leave him and vanish into one of the paintings."

"Maybe some closets or dioramas do lead to other worlds. Many authors have written about such possibilities," noted Matthew.

"Why are we talking about children's fiction anyway?" Joanne asked incredulously.

"All fiction is based on some aspect of reality, isn't it? At any rate, I'm hoping we will find something in this museum that will back up Joshua's story."

"What on earth?" exclaimed Joanne. A pigeon had landed on the bench's handrail right next to her and looked at her out of one eye.

"Maybe she's hungry." Joanne tore a piece of bread from her sandwich and held it out to the bird.

"Please be careful. That pigeon might be carrying any number of diseases. And what makes you think it's a female?" asked Matthew.

"She looks like a female. Oh, and I prefer to think of them as rock doves," said Joanne.

The pigeon did not take the bread, and when Joanne and Matthew got up from the bench to return to the museum, she flew away.

When they arrived at the museum's steps, Joanne flinched when something swooshed past her. Another pigeon, or perhaps the same one, flew right through the front entrance into the Theodore Roosevelt Rotunda.

"Hey, you're supposed to check in with security before entering the museum!" one of the guards hollered after the pigeon. An announcement was made over the speaker system, telling the staff to look out for the bird.

"Okay, so that was unusual," observed Matthew.

"Maybe she's just lost," noted Joanne.

"I doubt that! Pigeons know their way around. That's why people have employed them as messengers throughout history."

"Are you suggesting that a pigeon, flying into the museum, supports Joshua's story in some way?" Joanne asked in disbelief.

"Possibly!" answered Matthew.

Before they headed up to the office where Matthew had been staying, the Bradburys walked over to the Christmas tree to look for the paper whale that had been found with Noah's belongings. It had been put back on the tree, and when they found it Joanne became teary upon seeing the words "Noah, come home" written on it.

For the rest of the afternoon, the Bradburys tried to focus on their work without much success. After eating an early dinner, they left the office and walked down to the museum where they spent the evening searching through its galleries.

Everywhere, security personnel patrolled the halls with robotic dogs. They walked through the Hall of North American Mammals, expectantly, though nothing unusual happened. They then made their way to the Hall of New York State and the diorama of *An October Afternoon Near Stissing Mountain*. They stood side by side, gazing into the scenic view of the long-ago October day, waiting, for what they did not know.

"I might have hiked up Stissing Mountain while in summer camp as a kid. It's a small mountain, an hour or so from the city, in the Taconic range," said Matthew. "Maybe we should ride up there and look around."

"Taconic is a word of the Lenape Indians. If I recall correctly, it means something like 'In or through the Trees,'" Joanne remembered.

"I'm impressed you know that! Though I'm not sure if 'in the trees' would accurately describe it anymore," said her husband.

"I know I told you that my grandmother, the one who made our quilt, had ancestors who were Lenape," said Joanne.

"Yes, you did—and that she was also Dutch," said Matthew.

"Thanks to the two of us, Noah can stake a claim in many quarters of this world," Joanne said. She smiled at her husband, something she had not done much of since her son's disappearance.

Joanne and Matthew became very quiet as they continued gazing into the diorama. Just after they started to walk away, Matthew stopped and looked back.

"That's a trailhead," he announced.

"It's a what?" Joanne had no idea what he meant.

"When I was a kid at camp, we would go on day hikes. We would all gather to meet at what was called the trailhead. That right there is the start of a trail that leads somewhere," he explained.

"I'm tired, Matthew. I've had a long day—can we think more about this in the morning?" she pleaded.

When they returned to the office, though she was exhausted, Joanne lay in the fold-out bed unable to sleep. She looked about the snug little room. There was a glass-fronted bookcase that held microscopes, fossils, and century-old science textbooks. The latest computer tablet sat on a desk, next to an antique clock that glowed in the dark as it ticked off each passing second. There was a coffeemaker, a small refrigerator, and by the window, a rack bearing several plants growing from pretty ceramic pots.

It was a safe and quiet space where everything seemed rational. Through the window, light from a street lamp entered and fell across the wall. A siren shrieked, and police drones softly hummed overhead in the night sky. Joanne listened to her husband breathing as he slept. She was very concerned about him. Noah's disappearance and the immense pressure to find a cure for the tree disease were both taking their toll. She now feared that the stress he was under was interfering with his ability to think clearly and rationally. As Joanne worried about this, her own thinking grew fuzzy, and soon she too was asleep.

She did not sleep for very long. In the middle of the night, Joanne woke up when she felt something brush against her face. It was probably just an annoying stray hair. Still, she sat up and checked the bed for bugs. As she did, she noticed that the room was filled with a pale light as if the sun were just rising. Her eye caught a movement, a flutter of bright sunshine by the door. When she looked at it closely, she could not believe her eyes. Flying across from her, bathed in a golden light, was what appeared to be the ghost of a monarch butterfly.

A real live monarch butterfly had not been spotted outside a sanctuary for decades. Joanne got dressed and unlocked the door, for it seemed to her that the butterfly was asking to be let out. She followed the fairylike creature into the hallway, while her husband remained asleep. Along corridors, past closed doors, and down flights of stairs, she followed the butterfly into the dinosaur halls. The beautiful creature flew into one of the galleries and landed on the majestic skull of a triceratops.

After entering the gallery, Joanne stopped and stared. Gathered all over the ancient skeletons, slowly pulsing their delicate, brilliantly colored wings, were all kinds of butterflies.

For her doctoral program in entomology, Joanne had purchased an application for her computer that displayed moving, three-dimensional images of all kinds of insects. At first she thought the images she was seeing were created by the same application. But then one of the small yellow beings landed on her forearm.

The butterflies were real. Where had they come from? There were so many species, with wings covered in different kaleidoscopic designs. Among the crowd were red admirals, yellow swallowtails, and blue metalmarks. Joanne gazed in awe at a white butterfly, posing atop the jagged incisors in a jaw that once belonged to who knew what type of monster.

"Noah, are you here?" Joanne called out. "Tessa, please tell me where you are!"

The monarch butterfly flew around Joanne before stopping and hovering a few inches in front of her nose. She stared cross-eyed at the otherworldly being, before realizing that she was again being asked to follow. The yellow and black creature led the parade of ethereal beings down the stairs to the museum's main entrance where a forest of trees, plants, and flowers now grew, surrounding the dinosaurs Barosaurus and Allosaurus.

Standing on a bench, looking at Joanne, was the pigeon she had seen earlier that day in the park. The bird was perched next to a rolled-up piece of rough-looking paper that appeared to be made from tree bark. When Joanne walked up to her, the bird cooed and flapped her wings. Picking up the rough paper, Joanne unrolled it and saw, painted in bright yellow, a picture of the sun above the words *Happy New Year*.

Startled awake, Joanne Bradbury sat up on the fold-out bed and looked around the office in confusion. Her husband was still asleep beside her; and on the desk across the room, the glowing face of the antique clock told her that in two hours the sun would rise. As the fog of sleep dissipated, she regained her bearings and realized that her nighttime sojourn with the monarch butterfly had been only a dream.

# Part Three: The River

# Chapter 15

Noah remained submerged in the cold river, waiting for the man and hound, who hovered nearby, to leave the area. By the time they did, rejoining the other hunters who had moved their search further along the river, Noah had slipped into unconsciousness. He was about to disappear beneath the water's surface, when he heard a muffled voice, sounding distant and full of static, call out his name.

"Wake up, wake up," Noah's own inner voice coached. "You can do it."

Slowly and deliberately, Noah worked to lift himself up from the murky depths of water and sleep, until his eyes were suddenly flooded with brightness. Trying to regain his vision, he squinted at an indiscernible image that appeared above him. Encircled by a halo of hazy light, the image shimmered before solidifying into the form of an elderly man. As sleep battled to drag Noah back, the man fought to pull him in the opposite direction.

"You must try and help me, Noah. I cannot do this alone," said the elderly man, who struggled to lift him from the frigid waters.

Though weak and groggy, Noah took hold of the edge of what was a canoe. Kicking his legs, he lifted his torso up from the water, while the man took hold of his shoulders and pulled. After a great deal of effort, Noah rolled over the canoe's side and into its belly like a wet sack of sand.

"We must keep you hidden," said the man. He wrapped a blanket around Noah and helped him crouch down in the narrow space.

Using a single paddle, the man turned the canoe around and aimed its bow toward the sun that would soon set in the pink and blue sky on the opposite shore. Just as the sun disappeared behind a hill, the bottom of the canoe crunched over many small pebbles and glided onto a beach. There a young man met them and carried Noah on his back, through the woods, to a village of dome-shaped dwellings.

The group entered one of the small homes, where they were greeted by an elderly woman. After being set down on the floor, Noah watched sleepily as the young man bowed to the older couple before leaving the house through the mat-covered doorway. The man then spoke to the woman in a language Noah did not understand. Immediately, she left the house and returned carrying a pot filled with heated water and herbs.

The woman helped Noah put his feet and ankles into the warm bath. As they soaked, they began to thaw, and Noah struggled to keep from crying out in pain. When the water cooled, he removed them from the bath, and the woman covered them with a greasy paste before wrapping them up in strips of warm cloth. She then brought him a bowl of soup that had been heating over the fireplace.

Noah had practically no appetite. After a few mouthfuls of the spicy meat broth, he placed the bowl down by his side. Trying to remain awake, he focused intently on the snapping fire. Soon, his mind strayed into alleys of disorder and the flames turned into orange waves that rolled over the logs. As they washed out toward him, Noah's eyes closed and his head fell heavily onto his chest.

When Noah awoke, he was alone, lying on a sleeping mat in the one-room dwelling. The early morning sunlight filtered through the mat-covered doorway and reflected off the bowl of water Noah had soaked his feet in the night before. The light shimmered in a sphere on a wall, right above the spot where Noah's pack, deerskin clothing, and beaver skin pelts sat in a pile on the floor.

Sitting up, Noah threw off the wool blanket he was wrapped in and discovered that he had been dressed in a beaded leather tunic. He recalled the events of the previous day: he had sprained an ankle; a boy had stolen his belongings, leaving him with an empty pack and a pile of beaver skin pelts; and a man, in whose home he had spent the night, had called him by name before pulling him from the river.

Noah's feet and legs were still covered by the bandages the woman had put on him the night before. Even though his left ankle felt numb and stiff, like a piece of wood, Noah tried to stand up. After taking a few steps, a sharp, searing pain shot through it and he fell to the floor. He sat for several minutes, waiting for the pain to subside. Once it did, he carefully put on the pair of leggings that had been left for him near the sleeping mat and crawled to the door of the small house.

Outside, the sky was blue and a few stubborn yellow leaves still clung to the branches of the surrounding trees. The air was crisp and cold, and there was a smell of cooking. Noah looked around for the man and woman who had helped him the night before, but they were nowhere to be seen. Crawling onto a sunny patch of ground, he sat and observed the activity in the village.

There were several women sitting around a large fire baking bread, while a group of toddlers danced around them. Nearby, some chatty teenage girls were sewing, and a few older children were sweeping and shaking out mats. There were only a few men to be seen, and they passed quickly through the area. No one in the village seemed to be aware of Noah's presence.

Noah was wondering if anyone could even see him when a young boy and dog walked up to him. The boy just stood and stared, but the dog began to bark and growl. Once again, Noah was reminded that dogs seemed to dislike him. Thankfully, one of the women turned around and scolded the two. The boy pulled the dog away and Noah retreated back into the house. Returning to the sleeping mat, he curled up in the blanket and fell asleep once more.

At midmorning, Noah awoke to find the elderly woman stooped over the fire. When she realized that Noah was awake, she brought him a bowl of hot cereal that was made from mashed corn and sweetened with maple syrup. With a much better appetite than the night before, Noah ate heartily and as he did, the elderly man entered the house with an armload of wood.

"How is ice trout this morning?" The man addressed Noah as he dropped the logs by the fire. "Too cold now for swimming."

Noah looked up at the man who had spoken in Noah's language.

"I'm better! Thank you for helping me," Noah said shyly. "While I was in the water, I thought I heard someone call out to me."

"I know you are not a fur thief," said the man with a smile.

"No, of course I'm not," replied Noah indignantly.

"You are Noah, named for the one our new neighbors believe saved Earth's animals during the great flood."

"So, you do know who I am. Taman must have told you about me."

"No, Taman learned of you from me. Do you not remember meeting me?" asked the elderly man.

Noah thought for a moment. "Oh, I do remember! Back in the museum, the actor dressed in costume who brought me to the bathroom—that was you!"

"My name is Etchemin, but everyone calls me Eti. My wife is named Ro. I am one who travels by canoe. I too can make my way across rivers of time," the man told him with a twinkle in his eye.

"Are you Taman's father?" asked Noah.

"I must look very old," laughed Eti. "He and I are friends! We work together to bring peace to our world and now hope back to yours."

"Did the animals think I could help them because my name is Noah? Noah is a pretty common name in my world."

"You are here because both your name and your spirit recall that great savior of animals," Eti smiled. "Now, no more talking. You must rest and heal so you may succeed in your mission. You will stay in our home while you grow strong."

Noah learned that Eti was a master builder of canoes. He was also the leader and father figure of his village, and his canoe-building enterprise was its economic center. Eti, and the people in his village, built both dugout and birchbark canoes, which were celebrated for their beauty and craftsmanship throughout the river valley.

For the next several days Noah rested and then, like everyone else in the village, he was given work to do. His assigned chore was one that allowed him to remain off his feet while his ankle healed. The people in the village were preparing all kinds of food for an autumn feast, to give thanks to the Great One for a bountiful harvest season. Noah, along with two other boys, was to help an older man shell hickory nuts and black walnuts.

The group worked outside in the cold November air. The older man, who had years of experience doing so, cracked the nuts' rock-like shells open with a hammer-like stone. Noah and the two boys then helped him take out the meat inside. It took about a week to shell all the nuts needed for the celebration. By the time the boys were finished, Noah's nails and fingers were red and raw. But after sampling both types of nuts, he decided it had been worth the effort to extract them.

In the evenings, Noah sat with Eti and Ro by the warm fire in their one-room house. Eti played a flute, while Ro, who was making something from the beaver pelts Noah had given her, sang along with him. Sometimes, the dome-shaped house would fill up with people from the village who would join them to tell stories and play music. One evening, a young couple about ten years older than Noah arrived. The man was a boat builder and had come to discuss a canoe that was being made for a new settler.

As Noah regarded the young man and his wife, he noticed a distinctive tattoo, shaped like the letter V, on the man's left cheek. Eti introduced Noah to the man whose name was Ahnu. He suggested that Noah might be of help to Ahnu, who, along with two other men, was working to finish the settler's canoe. After a week of taking nuts out of their shells, Noah, who was starting to walk once more, readily agreed.

# Chapter 16

On the morning Noah was to begin his new job, Ahnu came to collect him. They walked through the village and into the woods, to a clearing where birchbark canoes were being made. Noah and Ahnu stopped by a fire to keep warm, and watched an assembly line of people working at different stages in the canoe-making process.

One group of men soaked and softened tree boughs in heated water, before bending them into bow shapes. The curved boughs were given to another group, who fit them together and constructed the basic skeletal frame of a canoe. The frames were then turned over to a group of women on the other side of the clearing. Sitting around a large fire, the women sewed sheets of the waterproof birchbark onto their sides.

Noah could have spent all day watching the birchbark canoes being made, but Ahnu brought him to a second work area where a long, graceful canoe sat on a structure built from logs. This was the dugout that was being finished for the settler. While the birchbark canoes were made for travel along the river, the dugout could be used for traveling on the ocean. Noah walked around the canoe and admired the artwork carved into its hull. There was an image of a sun on its bow and of two sea turtles on each of its sides.

Though it was smaller than the dugout canoe in the museum, it too was impressive to behold. Noah learned from Eti that this canoe had been made from the single trunk of a white pine tree. A hole had been burned into its center, after which the charred wood was scraped out to create a hollow space for seating. The hull of the canoe was then shaped and the artwork Noah admired carved into its wood. The men were almost finished sanding the boat and would soon apply an oil to its surface to seal and protect it.

For the rest of the day, Noah helped Ahnu and the men by handing them the supplies they needed as they worked. While Noah was happy to be helping in any way he could, on his second morning of work he asked Ahnu if he could help sand or rub oil onto the boat's hull. Ahnu, however, informed him there had been a change of plans, and that neither of them would be working on the canoe that morning.

"Today, you and I will test one of the new canoes out on the river. We must be sure it is strong enough to travel over the water," Ahnu told him.

"Isn't it too cold to be out on the river now? What if the canoe is not strong enough?"

"Don't worry! We will not sink."

"I'm not worried, it's just that I don't know anything about operating a canoe. The only time I've ever been in one was when Eti pulled me from the river," Noah replied.

"Manning a canoe is not easy, but you are a fast learner," Ahnu tried to persuade Noah.

"Isn't there someone who knows more about canoes than I who can help?"

"Etchemin has requested that you help test the canoe," said Ahnu, who raised his hands and shrugged his shoulders after he spoke.

"Why would Eti want me to help?"

"That is a question Eti must answer."

Noah understood that he had no choice but to do as Eti asked. With the help of Ahnu's co-worker, they carried the newly made birchbark canoe to the rocky beach. After Noah and Ahnu climbed into the canoe, the young man pushed it into the water. As they glided into the river, Ahnu began to teach Noah how to use the paddle.

The paddle worked the way Noah's hands did when he swam. Its movement, pulled the water back and propelled the canoe forward. To do so, one hand was positioned at the paddle's top and pushed forward, while the hand holding the paddle's middle pulled back. After each stroke, the paddle was turned sideways, so its flat surface would not slow the boat down.

While they practiced paddling, Noah tucked his chin into the warmth of his borrowed bearskin cloak. Both he and Ahnu sat in the canoe as still as statues. Any careless movement could capsize the small craft and land them both in the freezing water. After his recent experience, Noah wanted none of that. Instead of worrying about this, though, Noah focused on the peaceful sound the water made when it dripped from the paddle back into the river after each stroke.

When they returned safely to shore, Noah was relieved. They were pulling the boat onto the beach when Noah looked up at Ahnu and remembered where he had seen him. The marking on Ahnu's cheek was identical to that of the man in the canoe that had passed by Noah on the beach when he'd first arrived at the river. Noah remembered how the man had briefly glanced his way. Had Ahnu been the one to tell Eti of Noah's presence on the river? Perhaps the two men with him that day had been the settlers now buying the dugout canoe.

That night by the fire, Eti told Noah that Ahnu and two other men would leave in a week's time to deliver the dugout canoe to its new owner on Mannahatta Island. They would leave just after the arrival of the new moon and the village's celebration. The men would be traveling in two canoes. After leaving the dugout canoe with the settler, the men would return to the village in the birchbark canoe. Eti explained that the safest and fastest way for Noah to reach the island would be for him to travel with them.

For the next several days, Ahnu continued to teach Noah how to man the birchbark canoe. At night, Noah sat with Ro and Eti, warming himself by the fire in their small home. Eti told Noah all about the river, how its tides moved back and forth between the sea and the mountains, and how its dangerous currents could sink a canoe as they collided and competed with one another. One cold evening, as Ro worked on a garment she was making from the beaver skins, Eti told Noah all that he knew about the tree Noah was searching for.

"It is believed that the Grandmother Oak resides near the island's southern tip, where the two rivers meet the sea. There, the presence of the Great One is most strongly felt. Long ago, it was a quiet place, but now it is filled with new voices. The Grandmother Oak honors the son she lost by bearing an acorn that inherits her gift of healing. This acorn appears once every twelve years, and will only be released during an autumn snowfall, just before the arrival of the winter solstice. It is this seed that you must obtain and bring back to your own time."

"I thought I could find any one of her acorns," said Noah.

"This one acorn must be found this season. If it is not, we must wait another twelve years. By then the tree may no longer exist. During our celebration to honor the Great One, we will pray for an early snowfall, for you will not receive the tree's acorn without it," Eti told him solemnly.

"If the tree likes snow so much, why would she let her offspring be taken into a world where there isn't any?" asked Noah.

"As the young sapling works to heal the Earth, I hope it will work to bring back the snow," said Eti.

"My grandfather said he once saw snow when he was a kid in the mountains where he lives. It didn't stay long though. I have only seen it in a tree sanctuary. Some scientists are trying to recreate a cold climate within their sanctuaries, hoping that it will help the trees fight off their disease."

"Is that working?" asked Eti.

"I don't think so," Noah answered.

"Our season of snow cannot be recreated. It is a long season and a harsh one. Yet, it is a season of great beauty that brings rest and peace to many, including our trees. The snow cleanses our waters and helps our Earth grow her green treasures in spring."

"Eti, back in the museum, why didn't you tell me who you were? Couldn't you have brought me to the other side of the diorama?" asked Noah.

"Ah, only your spirit guide can lead you to another time and place," answered Eti.

"Are you telling me the wolf is my spirit guide? Are you sure it's not the whale?" asked Noah incredulously. "The wolf chased me all over the museum and then stole my backpack."

"The wolf led you into our world," noted Eti.

"But it was Taman who met me there. Why didn't you meet me there as well?"

"Taman is a much younger man than I and the only teacher you needed," Eti laughed softly. "After we met in the museum, there seemed no need for us to meet again. Then I learned from Ahnu that he had seen a boy who the hunters believed was a fur thief."

"I remember seeing Ahnu on the river," Noah told him. "Eti, since dogs have never liked me, I can't imagine a wolf being my spirit guide. Even here, in the village, a dog growled at me."

"That dog growls at everyone, including me," laughed Eti.

"When I was a little kid, there was a shepherd at the institute where I live, who was being trained as a security dog. When her trainer was with her, she was friendly and he let me play with her. Then one day, for no reason at all, she bit me."

Noah showed Eti the scar on his arm.

"The wolf marked you as one of his own through his descendant," Eti proclaimed. "The wolf is a most admirable creature. As a hunter, he is intelligent and fierce; yet to his mate and those he loves, he is faithful and kind. His spirit will help you be brave and strong as you make your way to the Great Oak or to the one I like to call *The Tree of Snow.*"

Just then Ro got up from her sewing and smiled mischievously. She reached up and took two ceramic jars down from a shelf along the wall. Reaching into one, she took out a handful of dried corn kernels and tossed them into the fireplace. From the second jar, she poured maple syrup into a small bowl. The kernels popped into what looked like fluffy, snow-white flowers. For the remainder of the evening, they sat by the fire, eating popcorn dipped in maple syrup, as Noah struggled to put the inevitable fact of his journey out of his mind.

The music Eti played on his flute that night filled Noah with sadness. He watched Eti gaze at his wife through eyes that, though tired and aged, sparkled with happiness. His wife's eyes glittered back as she smiled broadly like a young girl. Though Ro had never been able to have children of her own, she was regarded as the matriarch of her village. Her people loved her and her husband as one loved parents and grandparents. And now, though he had only known them a short while, Noah loved them as well.

Noah felt a deep sadness over his impending departure from them. Once again, he grappled with the harsh reality that any journey, whether it be along a winding trail, over a river or through time, eventually leads to a separation. As it was with Taman, Eti and Ro would always be a part of him. Still, that didn't make it any easier.

Later that night, the melody of Eti and Ro's music filled Noah's dream. In it, he stood under a dome-shaped cathedral of deep cobalt-blue sky, crowded with stars and spiraling galaxies. They swirled overhead, full of brilliant color—yellow, orange, red, purple, and green. They were enormous and so close that he was afraid they would fall and crush him.

"We don't move in a straight line, we spiral and move in circles." Noah thought he'd heard one say.

Then Noah understood something. Traveling along a circle allows for the possibility of return. For the first time since entering this world, Noah awoke with a feeling of peace.

The morning of the autumn celebration was a beautiful one. The sun shone in the blue sky, though the air was brisk and chilly. Noah's ankle was healing well, and he walked comfortably, feeling the hard earth beneath his moccasins as he made his way to the clearing. There, he helped Ahnu and a group of young men assemble tables made from logs and rough planks of wood. They were placed around the clearing between the canoes, all of which, even the unfinished ones, were decorated with fall leaves, berries, and corn husks. After the work was done, everyone painted his face with important symbols and dressed in their finest clothes, and Noah did the same.

The feast began in the early evening and lasted well into the night. The tables were loaded with roast turkey, deer and bear meat, baked sturgeon, and piles of oysters. There were roasted chestnuts, squash, corn, and beans. The meal was served with water, beer, and later herbed tea. For dessert, there were pumpkin puddings baked in their shells, sweet bread and pastry made from berries, maple syrup, and the hickory and black walnuts Noah had helped shell. Noah had never eaten such wonderful food.

When the meal was finished, everyone gathered around a huge fire in the clearing's center, whose sparks shot halfway up to the stars. Musicians played their instruments while people danced in a blurry of color. They lifted their voices in song, sending prayers that radiated out like the fire's light into the dark and cold night. As they did, Noah stood alone and solemnly sent his silent prayer up to the heavens. He remained watching the festivities until his eyes began to close. The following morning, he awoke on his sleeping mat in Eti's small round-shaped house for the last time.

That afternoon, the two canoes, which had been filled with supplies, including food left over from the great feast, waited for their passengers on the same pebbly beach where Noah had arrived. Their crew would leave at sunset and travel throughout the night with the tide as it moved out to sea. The recent new moon would cast little light and allow them to remain unseen as they traveled through dangerous areas along the river.

Noah arrived for the next part of his journey bundled up in new clothing Ro and other women in the village had made for him: a warm pair of leather boots, mittens, a hat, and a warm mantle that Ro had made from raccoon fur and the beaver skin pelts he had given her. Noah had not suspected she had been making something for him. Bravely, he stepped into the birch-bark canoe and kneeled at its front, grateful that he would be traveling in the same boat as Ahnu.

As they set off, Noah turned back to look at Eti and Ro who were standing side by side on the beach. Ro was smiling and waving to him. Noah smiled and waved back to her before turning around to face the river. When he had thanked her for the beautiful clothing she and her friends had made, he had tried to keep his eyes from spilling tears. But now he needed one of his new mittens to wipe them from his face, so they wouldn't be able to freeze there.

# Chapter 17

One week after they returned from the ceramics worksite, Tessa learned that she and Ayanna were to help Nora and one of Nora's sisters sell pottery at a large farmer's market. It was the last market of the autumn season, and tradesmen from all over New Netherland were expected to attend. Early on a chilly, overcast morning, they set off in the small wagon. Nora and her sister sat at the wagon's front while Tessa and Ayanna sat in the back among the cups, bowls, oil lanterns, candle holders, and vases.

When they arrived at the farm, Tessa and Ayanna helped set up a display of ceramics on the ground around the wagon before being allowed to explore the market. Nora very generously gave them each a shell bead to spend on whatever they wished. Everywhere there were wooden tables and carts laden with all kinds of merchandise: feather beds, woven rugs, blankets, baskets, copper pots, spices, milled grains, and cheese. As

Tessa and Ayanna walked through the market, Tessa could not take her eyes off the large families of settlers.

The settlers looked very much like the pilgrims depicted in one of the history books owned by the library at Tessa's school back at the institute. They all seemed as somber as the long, dark clothing they wore, except for three girls, who pointed at Tessa and began to giggle and whisper as she and Ayanna walked by them.

"What is their problem?" asked Tessa. The girls could have been Daniela and her friends back at school, if not for their long dresses and white bonnets.

"They don't know you," Ayanna told her. "And remember, you must not tell anyone who you are."

Tessa knew that she looked different, not only from Ayanna, but from everyone else in this world. She figured that the girls were probably laughing at her because of her hair. She had been doing a fairly good job of distributing what was left of it around the bald pink patches of her scalp. But now a downy new under-growth was inexplicably growing back. Without the constant mirrors that existed in her world, she couldn't see what it looked like, but the whole thing felt like an uncontrollable mess.

Perhaps the girls, whose own hair was covered, were simply reacting to the fact that Tessa's hair was exposed. In fact, most of the settler women were wearing bonnets. It occurred to Tessa that one of the crisp, white caps might serve as a replacement for her now disintegrated kerchief. One would certainly hide her unruly hair, and she liked the way they looked on the girls: how strands of their blond hair escaped from beneath them and flew prettily about their faces. Tessa asked Ayanna to walk with her to a table where two Dutch women were selling fabrics along with the pretty head coverings.

"How does this look?" Tessa asked, as she adjusted the white cap on her head and tied it beneath her chin.

"I wouldn't wear one!" Ayanna replied.

Tessa took the bonnet off. Though she couldn't see how it looked, it just didn't feel right. Instead, she began looking through the fabrics on the table for something out of which to make a new kerchief. Unlike the synthetic, lightweight textiles of her own world, the fabrics on the table were made from natural fibers. Tessa had never seen such beautiful cloth. She looked at a piece of white linen longingly, but it was too stiff and heavy for a headscarf.

"I am going to make this into a shawl," Ayanna announced. She gave her shell bead to the Dutch women for a piece of beautiful blue wool, the color of an early evening sky.

The girls were walking back to the wagon when Tessa spotted a table where a young couple was selling remedies for skin ailments. While Ayanna returned to her mother and aunt, Tessa walked to the table and spoke to the couple. They told her that their product not only soothed burns and rashes, but also promoted fingernail and hair growth. The remedy, they confided, was made from a unique mixture of herbs and honey.

Back at the institute, Tessa had tasted honey with her science class when they visited a beehive at one of the sanctuaries. The sweet, syrupy substance was a rare treat in Tessa's world, and she readily gave the couple her bead for one of the jars. But when she returned to the wagon and showed everyone her purchase, Nora shook her head dismally.

"My mother thinks those traders are thieves. Honey and herbs are easy to find, and while they will soothe burns and rashes, they will not make hair grow," Ayanna told her. "But don't worry. She didn't like my purchase either. She threatened to buy a settler's spinning wheel so that I can learn to spin and weave wool for our whole family."

"But that would be great!" Tessa replied. Ayanna looked at her without saying anything.

As they headed back to the village, everyone seemed content. Nora and her sister had traded many pieces of pottery for needed supplies. Ayanna was thrilled with her wool and even if Tessa had been deceived, she too was happy with her purchase. She planned to put drops of the skin remedy onto her hot cereal every morning. She would use it sparingly though, so it would last for as long as possible.

It was now late autumn in the world of the past and the nights were becoming shorter, darker, and very cold. One evening while everyone in the longhouse huddled by the fire, Tessa, who missed being in school, introduced the game of charades, thinking that the game might help Ayanna's younger brother and sister and many cousins learn English words.

"What am I?" Tessa called out, galloping and neighing, shaking her head until someone gave her the English word for "horse."

The game of charades became a big hit and Tessa and Ayanna began leading it each night after everyone had eaten dinner and done their chores. They acted out the parts of numerous animals and soon expanded their word list to include all kinds of things: food items, clothing, and actions such as walking and swimming. Other families in the village began to join them, and one clear evening, the crowd became so large that the game was held outdoors by a big fire.

One night after the word game was over, Tessa saw Nora and Ayanna arguing. She knew it had something to do with her as they both kept looking at her. Once again, she was afraid she had done something wrong.

"My mother says it is time for you to cut your hair," Ayanna informed her.

"Well, I don't know if I want to yet," answered Tessa, who was relieved to know that they hadn't been talking about anything more serious.

"I think it looks fine," said Ayanna. "But she says it looks terrible and that if you cut it, it will grow back and become strong."

"Everyone here has long hair, even the boys," Tessa said. "I would rather cut it when it grows out more. It will look strange otherwise."

When Ayanna relayed this information to her mother, Nora made a reply and then sighed in exasperation.

"She says it cannot look any stranger than it does now," Ayanna told Tessa.

Reluctantly, Tessa conceded and allowed Nora to cut the top layer of long, scraggly hair to an inch below the new undergrowth. Several of the children gathered around and watched solemnly as Tessa's hair fell to the ground. Though Ayanna tried to reassure her that it looked fine, Tessa could tell by the children's reaction that the haircut was a terrible one.

When Tessa and her family had gotten sick, she'd stopped caring about her appearance. Later, after she'd been placed in the foster home and returned to school, she was even grateful for looking horrible because everyone left her alone. She would retreat into her sketch pad, books, and well-imagined day-dreams. But since arriving in this world, she had begun to care about what she looked like. Here, she was surrounded by people, and there was even someone she especially admired, someone she wished would think she was pretty.

That night, Tessa cried into her sleeping mat. She thought about how her mother would cut her hair when there was little money to go to the salon. After leaving this world, maybe it would be possible to return to a time before she and her fam-ily had become ill. Here she was in a world with people who had lived hundreds of years before anyone in her own family had even been born. So why couldn't she return to her own family? She had always believed they still existed somewhere else. But all this speculation brought her little comfort. They were not here.

As Tessa waited for sleep, she comforted herself by imagining that she was walking through the woods with Elan. She had not seen him since the morning they walked beneath the fiery autumn trees, and now the tree's branches were bare. As she drifted off to sleep, they continued walk-ing together through her dream, on a path that led to an old house. Inside, Tessa knew that her grandparents, parents, and sister—all now absent in her own time—were waiting. When they reached the house and stepped through its front door, those absent loved ones greeted Tessa and Elan, as Tessa fell into a deep and sound sleep.

A few days later, on a cold November afternoon, Tessa and Ayanna were sitting beneath the ash tree sewing leather pouches, when the form of a man appeared over the rise in the valley. Ayanna dropped her sewing and without a word jumped up and took off in flight. Tessa squinted as she watched Ayanna run across the brown grass to meet the man. Ayanna threw her arms about him and together they began walking back toward the village. When they reached her, Tessa saw that the man looked similar to Elan, only much older. The man nodded to her as he walked by, but neither he nor Ayanna said anything.

Tessa had been waiting so long for Ayanna's father to return with Noah. If the man with Ayanna was her father, Taman, then why wasn't Noah with him? Tessa imagined all kinds of horrible possibilities. Perhaps Noah had been hurt by an animal. What if Taman had harmed or abandoned him and Ayanna had known about this? Had Ayanna and the rest of her family tricked Tessa into believing that both she and Noah were safe? For most of the night, Tessa remained awake feeling distrustful of everyone sleeping around her. She had only just fallen asleep when Ayanna woke her early in the morning.

"My father wishes to speak with you," Ayanna whispered.

Quietly, so as not to wake anyone else up, Tessa followed Ayanna out of the house. They walked along a wooded trail that led to the small hut Elan had built, the one where Noah had stayed on the night of his arrival. Inside, Ayanna's father was sitting by the fireplace, and he motioned for Tessa to sit across from him. When he looked at her with kind eyes and smiled, Tessa immediately began to cry. She tried to stop herself but her homesickness and fear for Noah, even the relative meaninglessness of her shorn hair, had all gathered into one large thunderhead that poured out uncontrollably.

"I hear from my children that you are strong and capable," Taman told her.

"No, I am not!" Tessa gasped for breath as she spoke. "Do you know where Noah is? Ayanna told me that he was with you."

"Noah is safe and well. He has embarked on an important journey, and you are here to help him," Taman answered.

Tessa listened as Taman told her all about Noah's quest for the Great Oak: how he must find it and return to their world of the future with one of its acorns before the arrival of the winter solstice. "You are here to help Noah and the Great Oak heal your world, by gathering seeds from our trees," he told her.

"I've been collecting seeds from all kinds of plants," Tessa said, looking up with surprise. "I will show you what I've found so far!"

As Tessa went to retrieve her birchbark box, she felt like a different person than the one she had been upon entering the hut. Now she knew why both she and Noah were here. Though Tessa couldn't be with Noah on his journey, the fact that he was still here and safe was an enormous relief.

When Tessa returned, she handed her birchbark box to Taman.

"We are fortunate that you began to do this early. Such strong, healthy seeds are harder to find this late in the season," Taman told her as he examined them. "If the acorn takes root in your world, then you may bring seeds from our world back to your own time."

"What if Noah is unable to find the acorn? Can I still go home?" Tessa asked in a shaky voice.

"You may return home, but without the seeds. They will be of no use in your world and will remain here," said Taman.

Tessa nodded to indicate that she understood. Once again, she was proud of her intuition, this time for having told her to begin collecting seeds.

"There is one more thing," said Taman. "The seeds must be carried into your world in something you have made with your own hands."

"When Ayanna and I helped Nora with her pottery, I made a jar that will hold the seeds," Tessa told him.

"A jar will be fine," Taman smiled.

Then something occurred to Tessa. "The cougar who led me here, did she know about Noah's mission?"

"The animals chose you and Noah for this mission. Though they do not use words, animals know many things. Earth is their home too, and you are both here to help them as well."

One evening, despite the cold, the people from the village gathered outside by a big fire to play music and dance. Bundled up in a fur wrap, Tessa sat by herself and watched them, as she had the people in her own world sing and dance on the hot city streets. Nearby, she saw that Taman too sat alone, gazing soberly up at the star-filled sky. Tessa knew that, like her, he was thinking about Noah. Bravely, she walked over to him.

Taman greeted Tessa and began to tell her about the constellations overhead. He pointed to the starry forms of a bison, a bear, and a lion all animals Tessa had seen in the American Museum of Natural History. But Tessa could not find them in the night sky. Then Taman pointed to one of the brightest stars in the Milky Way. In Tessa's world that star was known as Sirius or the Dog Star. Taman was trying to help Tessa locate a constellation near Sirius, when someone interrupted him.

"The Great Chief is my favorite," said a familiar voice referring to the constellation also known as Orion. "When he arrives in the night sky, he brings with him the heavy snow of winter."

Tessa felt something leap inside her. How was it that she had not seen Elan return? She looked up at him as he began to retell a legend that he had heard as a child, from a people who had once visited from far away.

"In the Great Chief's belt there are two canoes. They are racing along the river, trying to catch that big salmon," said Elan pointing to Sirius. "The smaller canoe is the one who looks to be winning. It just might be the one who will reach the salmon first."

As Tessa listened to him, her heart raced with excitement and a new sense of hope. She was so happy to see him again.

There was a lot of work to be done to prepare for the cold winter months ahead. Still, with Nora's help, Tessa found time to build two more lidded jars from the clay they had collected earlier in the fall. The late autumn passed quickly and soon a bitter cold that Tessa had never imagined possible rattled the bare-branched trees. In the mornings, while doing her chores, her breath billowed a white smoke into the air. One morning, she stepped outside to find that overnight a white powder had fallen, covering everything in sight, transforming the world.

Tessa scooped up a handful of the icy crystals and examined them. After enclosing them tightly in her fist, she opened her palm to find that they had dissolved. Ayanna had warned her that once the ground turned white it would remain so until it was time for little green shoots to poke their noses up from the mud. Ayanna's family had many words for it, but in Tessa's language the substance that had not been seen in her own world for decades was remembered as "snow."

# Chapter 18

It took Noah and the three men almost a week to reach the Island of Many Hills, where Noah now stood looking out at the two rivers merging into one. A trio of yellow leaves swirled in a whirlpool of wind about his ankles as he breathed in the cold, damp air, now tinged with salt from the river's brackish waters. He had spent the past two nights in a shelter the men had helped him make, surviving on the food they had left for him, the remainder of a sturgeon they'd caught and the last of the leftovers from the great feast.

Noah took the leather pouch that Ro had made out of his pack. He had kept it there since Ahnu and the men presented it to him just before they left to deliver the canoe. Filled with several purple and white beads that Ro had collected from people in her village, it was meant to protect Noah and bring him good luck. Spilling the wampum beads into the palm of his hand, he admired their color and shape. They had been made from quahog shells and were used throughout New Netherland as a form of currency. Noah returned the beads to the pouch and tied its leather cords around his neck. From now on he would wear the pouch against his chest.

As Noah looked at the two rivers, a nagging voice within urged him to hurry up and be on his way. For the past two days, he had rested. Though he was at least a decade younger than the other men, he had worked as hard as they had, paddling for almost an entire week, through pain and exhaustion. As he dismantled his shelter and cleaned up his campsite, he felt the resulting soreness in his muscles. But the discomfort was worth the pride he felt in himself.

The two canoes had begun their trip along the great beltway of river, beneath an inky-blue, star-filled sky, not as competitors in pursuit of salmon but as a team. Noah and Ahnu manned the smaller birchbark canoe while their two companions manned the dugout. All through the nights on the river, they had been surrounded by nocturnal life: coyotes howled, owls screeched, and the occasional large fish would startle them by unexpectedly surfacing and splashing them with icy water. One night, two unseen animals growled ferociously as they engaged in a horrifying battle. When one let out a bloodcurdling shriek, Noah turned to look at Ahnu.

"Animals must eat," Ahnu had said. The battle had been followed by an eerie silence that spread across the river.

The incident that left them all most shaken happened on their third night of travel. A dense fog had blown in from the ocean and settled on the river, surrounding the canoes and making it hard to see. Deciding that the safest thing to do would be to rest for the night, the men in both boats put their paddles down and allowed the wind and the river's outgoing current to carry them along. They were floating peacefully when just ahead, a small bright star pierced through the dark fog.

As the star drew near, the triangular bow of the large sailing vessel to which it was attached emerged from the low-lying cloud. The ship's bow sliced through the water and headed directly toward the dugout canoe. Noah and Ahnu watched in horror as the two men frantically maneuvered the settler's new canoe out of the ship's way. The huge vessel just missed them, and as it moved past them, both canoes bounced over waves from its trailing wake.

The following afternoon, a cold icy rain began to fall. Still shaken from the near disaster of the night before, the men all agreed to remain at their daytime campsite for the night. They had passed through the more dangerous areas of the river valley, and soon the nighttime tide would be incoming and move against them. Though it was still risky, they decided to begin paddling on the river during daylight hours. Noah was grateful to be awake and moving beneath the sun again, even if it cast little warmth and meant they would have to work against the current for a part of each day.

By the end of their first day of travel, Noah couldn't tell if they had made any progress. When they were traveling by night, he was able to see changes in the landscape each morning. The narrow river of the night before would have widened, the rolling hills along the shoreline would have flattened. Once they began traveling during the daytime, these changes happened in increments, and sometimes it seemed as if they were making no progress at all. During the last days of their journey, the dramatic cliffs to their right continued, on and on, and Noah wondered if the canoes had remained in the same spot the entire time. But they had been making progress all along, and two days ago, they'd arrived at the tip of the Great Island.

Before leaving his campsite, Noah looked out at the river. Along its shoreline, the last remnants of autumn color reflected in the water. The river had brought him to safety on two occasions and had indeed been his friend. After packing his meager belongings, making sure he left nothing behind, Noah turned away, and for the time being, parted from the river's company. He walked along a path in search of the inland trail that Ahnu told him would take him to the other end of the island, to the Dutch settlement of New Amsterdam. It was there that the two rivers met the sea and where Eti said the tree was thought to reside.

The trail Noah found was more like a rugged road. It was rutted by the tracks and punctures of wagon wheels and horse hooves, and when Noah walked onto it he could feel the road's hard ridges of mud through his leather boots. Tucking his chin into his raccoon and beaver-skin mantle, he avoided eye contact with the travelers he passed. Some were on horseback while others, such as a man and a woman carrying a bucket filled with oysters, were on foot. At the sound of a rumbling noise behind him, Noah turned to see two young men pulling a cart filled with logs. They were taking turns drinking from a flask while laughing loudly. Noah stepped into the woods by the road to let them pass and felt relieved when they paid no attention to him.

It occurred to Noah that the road he was following was situated where Broadway, the famous New York street, would be one day. Back in his own world, this same area was filled with businesses, apartment buildings, schools, and a hospital. He was considering how drastically the region would change, when he suddenly felt a vibration underfoot. Ducking behind a low wall of granite rocks which bordered and marked a farm's fields he watched a horse-drawn wagon approach lazily from around a bend in the road.

The wagon was filled with what looked like burlap sacks and was driven by a distracted-looking middle-aged man. Rallying what remained of his strength, Noah ran up to it from behind, grabbed hold, and pulled himself onto its back. Crawling into a space between brown sacks full of milled grains, Noah held tightly onto the wagon as it bumped and rolled over the hilly landscape.

The wagon passed large boulders, ponds, streams, farms, and a small settlement, while always remaining in the company of trees. As it traveled southeast, Noah curled up and fell asleep against the jostling sacks of grain. He slept peacefully and soundly until the wagon came to a stop and someone roughly shook him. Opening his eyes, he saw the angry driver glaring at him.

"I'm sorry, sir! I didn't think you'd mind if I caught a ride with you. I didn't do any damage to the grain sacks," Noah apologized.

"It is not for me to grant forgiveness. You must wait here for me, boy," said the man.

"Can you tell me where we are?" asked Noah. But the driver had already walked hurriedly away.

Still disoriented from sleep and not thinking clearly, Noah remained sitting in the wagon, waiting for the driver to come back. He looked about at the small busy town. The scene reminded him somewhat of an illustration he'd once seen in an old book about Thanksgiving. Many of the people were dressed like pilgrims, while others were dressed as natives. Unlike the pilgrims' small village, however, this town was more complex and busier, filled with many well-designed and fine-looking buildings made from wood and stone. Men, women, children, dogs, horses, and even some unfettered chickens roamed through its center.

When the driver returned, he brought a man with him who was attired in what looked to be a military uniform.

"Welcome to New Amsterdam, son. You are under arrest and you must come with me," said the man firmly.

There was no point in objecting. Noah followed the man into what he learned was New Amsterdam's town hall. There he was accused not of hitching a ride as he'd expected, but of thievery. All his clothing, his boots, and pack, along with the cherished mantle and bead-filled pouch that Ro had made him, were taken away, stolen this time by officials who were ironically accusing him of stealing. They gave him a drab convict's gown to wear, made from a scratchy material much like the wagon's grain sacks. To replace his boots, they gave him a pair of wooden shoes that were impossible to walk in. For the time being, though, it didn't seem that he would be doing much walking.

An official took Noah to an underground cellar where he locked him in for the night. Noah sat down on the cell's bed, a lumpy mattress resting on a platform of woven ropes tied to a wobbly wooden frame. He was devastated about losing everything Ro had made for him. Despite his distress, he tried to remain as calm and serene as he imagined Taman would, had he been robbed and accused of a crime he didn't commit. Noah spent the long, cold night wrapped in a rough and itchy woolen blanket, thankful only for the fact that he was alone and could rest his aching shoulders and ankle.

# Chapter 19

Early the next morning, Noah had just fallen asleep when the sound of someone unlocking the cellar door woke him. He sat up on the bed and watched a young woman, carrying a covered basket and wearing a long black cloak, enter his cell. She spread the basket's contents, a stew made from corn and turkey meat, bread, and a flask of beer, onto the rickety table and then sat down on the room's only chair.

"May the Lord forgive you your sins," she said, bowing her head in prayer.

"I have done nothing wrong," Noah replied.

"A boy who fit your description was seen stealing furs from the West India Trading Company. Were your garments not made from them?"

"I haven't stolen any furs."

"You were hiding in the farmer's wagon. Did you not steal from him as well?" she asked.

"I stole a ride from him, but that was all. I am not a thief."

"I prepared this food for your breakfast. It will give you strength." The young woman gestured toward the table.

"Thank you, but I'm not hungry." Noah turned away from the young woman and curled up into himself as Tessa had done on the bus.

"Better to have been caught by the gentlemen of New Amsterdam than to remain among the merciless gang of thieves with whom you work," lectured the woman.

"I don't work with a gang of thieves. I told you, I'm not a thief," said Noah, staring coldly at the woman.

The woman solemnly returned Noah's gaze.

"A boy stole all of my things and left me with his pelts. I gave them to my aunt, and she made those garments for me." Noah felt as if Ro were a family member and so forgave himself for the falsehood.

"You say a boy left you with the pelts you wore. Did you know that the pelts were stolen?" asked the young woman whose voice had softened.

"No, I thought he left them to pay for my fur wrap and the supplies he took from me," said Noah.

"So, you were tricked into accepting stolen goods. You didn't know you should have returned them to the West India Trading Company."

"No, how would I know that?" asked Noah.

"My name is Elizabeth. Try to rest now. I will return tomorrow morning," she said, leaving the uneaten food but taking her basket. She closed and locked the cellar door behind her.

When he was alone, Noah kicked and kicked at the locked door, though all he managed to accomplish by doing so was to hurt his foot. He wondered how long these people would keep him locked away. Noah wished the same phantom who freed him from the bathroom back in the American Museum of Natural History would return to help him escape from this cell. He had learned about Colonial America and how "the good men of New Amsterdam" treated criminals, even underage ones. The good men were probably just as horrible, if not worse, than any gang of thieves.

It was late afternoon by the time Noah was hungry. The stew Elizabeth had left on the table had grown cold. Still it was good, and he devoured it along with the bread. Though the beer she'd left was bitter tasting, Noah did not object to drinking it. Later, he was glad he'd eaten the meal and was no longer hungry. A steely-eyed man brought him a porridge made from a mixture of mushy bread and beer for dinner. Noah took one bite of the food and spit it out. Though his stomach growled, he was unable to eat the meal.

Noah spent a second sleepless night shivering in the freezing cell, despite being wrapped up in the wool blanket. In the morning, when the cold-looking man returned, this time with some stale bread and moldy cheese, he informed Noah that in three days he was to have a hearing. Noah remembered reading about the West India Trading Company in his history class. Unlike Taman's community, the company didn't seem to care or have much respect for the animals whose furs they traded. Most animals were viewed merely as commodities, to be sold for profit to rich Europeans who would turn them into top hats and other vanity items.

For the next few days while Noah awaited trial, Elizabeth, thankfully, was the one who delivered his meals. She brought her sewing along with her, and while he ate the salty fish stew or corn and bread chowder she had made, she sat and talked with him. Though Noah could not tell her who he was or where he came from, he did tell her about his canoe trip along the river. Elizabeth, in turn, told him her own story.

Like Tessa, Elizabeth had lost her family as a child, by way of a deadly virus that had spread throughout the island where they lived. Her guardianship fell to her father's employer, and at age fourteen Elizabeth began working on his farm to pay him back for her care. In the spring of her sixteenth year, a ship from the West India Trading Company came to her island to trade fabrics and spices for sugar and tobacco. When a senior officer from the company admired Elizabeth and asked her guardian if she could be a part of their trade, her guardian consented. Elizabeth, an indentured slave, would now owe the tradesman for the years of care her guardian had given her.

Elizabeth had been devastated to learn that the tradesman's intention was to bring her to the new world. It meant she would have to leave her home and everyone she had ever known. During their voyage across the sea, her new owner became ill and just after they arrived in New Amsterdam, he died from a fever. Her indenture was then transferred to his employer, The West India Trading Company. The company, having no full-time work for Elizabeth, turned her over to a young man who worked for them and needed someone to help his pregnant wife.

Elizabeth assured a horrified Noah that her caretakers were a kind couple who regarded her as an employee, if not a family member. She had her own room in their house, and they paid her wages to clean, cook, and help care for their four young children. She told Noah that at times the West India Trading

Company did need her help on special assignments, which was how she came to be attending to him.

The morning of Noah's hearing was a cold and dreary one, made even more so when Elizabeth did not come to his cell. Instead, an officer arrived who bound Noah's hands and led him past a crowd that wore both the attire of Eti and Taman's people and of new settlers. When they arrived at the wall surrounding Fort Amsterdam, the officer led Noah through to a building where the trial would be held. Most of the spectators had to remain outside and wait to hear the fate of Noah and two other men, who were also charged with high crimes.

Inside the courthouse, Noah sat on a wooden bench and listened to the hearings of the other men. One was accused of forging a signature and the other of appearing drunk in public on a Sunday. Both were found guilty and received sentences unheard of in Noah's world. When it was time for his case to be heard, Noah focused on Taman's strength and demeanor, remembering his warning: not for any reason should you reveal your identity or mission to anyone who does not know your name.

Noah struggled to remain brave and calm. The driver of the wagon was the first to testify as to how he had found Noah. Then a second man, who Noah had never seen before, testified that he saw Noah stealing pelts belonging to the West India Trading Company.

"What is your name, son?" asked a judge.

"Joshua, sir! My name is Joshua," Noah replied.

"What say you to these charges, Joshua?" the judge asked.

"I am innocent of these charges. I did not steal any pelts," said Noah.

"From where did you get this item found on your person?" The judge held up Noah's fur mantle for all to see. "Is it not made from stolen furs?"

"The fur wrap was made from pelts a boy left with me after he took all my belongings. I didn't know he had stolen those pelts," said Noah, spotting Elizabeth among the gathered crowd. She seemed to nod her head and smile slightly.

"Tell me, who turned the pelts into this garment?" demanded the judge.

"My aunt made it for me. I needed a new wrap after the boy stole mine."

"Where are your parents?" asked the judge, who spoke English better than many in New Amsterdam.

"They do not reside in this world," Noah told him truthfully.

"An orphan, then...such is the kind recruited by these criminals," muttered the judge as he jotted down notes on a sheet of paper.

"And now, where and with whom do you reside?" asked the judge looking up at Noah.

"With my aunt and uncle in the mountains," Noah again lied, though reluctantly. He had wanted to remain as truthful as possible.

"Are you at work with fur thieves, son?"

"No, sir, I am not."

"What brought you to New Amsterdam?"

"I seek an honest trade, sir. Perhaps as the builder of canoes or boats," said Noah. A wave of laughter rippled throughout the room.

"Should you confess to your compliance with this gang of thieves, your sentence shall be lightened," offered the judge.

"I am not going to lie and confess to something I didn't do!" yelled Noah, on the verge of tears.

The judge sighed and said no more. It seemed it was not the answer he wished to hear. Just before the court recessed to determine Noah's fate, a man sitting among the throng of spectators raised his hand high.

"The boy wishes to build boats. I am in need of a shipbuilder," said the man. Again, laughter broke out among the crowd, and the man laughed with them.

"Or better still, an apprentice to work for my crew, your Honor, and this boy shall serve," the man shouted. "I shall see to it that this boy works to pay his debt to this honorable and pious company for any theft he may have committed. He shall learn the shipping trade and one day, should the good Lord be willing, he will become a productive member of society."

"We will consider your request, Master Giles," said the judge.

While the court deliberated his fate, Noah regarded the man who—though handsome in a gnarly, bearded sort of way—glared back at him with a cold stare. Some who had observed the proceedings expressed sympathy for the presumed orphan and believed there had been a lack of credibility in the testimony of at least one of the witnesses. Others, however, were convinced of Noah's guilt. When the judge announced that the offer made by Master James Giles had been accepted, both sighs of relief and angry objections were heard throughout the courtroom.

"This young rascal will repay the company for his theft by way of hard work. Through firm discipline, he will learn a useful trade, as he is set on a path toward redemption and good citizenship." The judge had delivered his decision.

# Part Four: Two Storms

# Chapter 20

Master James Giles was an Englishman who worked for the Dutch West India Trading Company, commanding a ship named *the Engel* that transported furs and other supplies between Europe and the new colonies. Having arrived back in New Amsterdam in early November, he and his crew had planned to stay in the colony only briefly, before continuing on to the Southern Settlements. Just before they were to set sail, however, they discovered that the ship's hull had been damaged.

Master Giles had asked his employer to postpone the voyage until springtime, but when the repair was made quickly, the company encouraged him to set sail by mid-December. The company argued that the Southern Settlements were in need of supplies. They further persuaded the master by likening him and his crew to a flock of migrating birds, who would fly south and remain where it was safe and warm throughout the winter. Noah, though he had not yet been told any of this, would do so as well.

Outside the courtroom, by the wall that surrounded Fort Amsterdam, Master Giles approached Noah who was still in the custody of law officials. The officer in charge of Noah stepped aside to allow the master to address his new apprentice privately.

"Greetings, my young friend. Soon we will board your ark of salvation. Shall we call you Noah?" the master laughed heartily.

Noah stared in disbelief upon hearing the master utter his real name.

"That is a bit of seafaring humor. I seem to remember you telling the judge that your name is Joshua something. Since I suspect you of telling falsehoods, I just might announce you as our ship's new Noah."

"My name *is* Noah."

"Well then, Noah, perhaps you are suited to the shipping trade after all. You will return with the officer to your current residence and pack your possessions. I expect you to immediately move into one of the lodgings where my crew is staying." The master slapped Noah on his back before walking briskly away.

The officer moved Noah out of the cell and brought him to an equally cold barn on a farm just outside of New Amsterdam. There, a friendly young crew member named Jasper was assigned the job of watching over him. While most of the crew set to work replenishing the ship's stores, Noah remained in the barn cleaning, unaware of the preparations being made. Crew members cut firewood, fetched barrels of beer and fresh water, and traveled to nearby farms to obtain bread, smoked meats, and sacks of grain, all of which would be loaded onto the ship.

One morning, Jasper brought Noah to the town's pretty church where clothing was being distributed to those crew members whose own meager wardrobes had failed them by falling apart, being outgrown, or in Noah's case by being just plain inappropriate. Jasper helped him pick out an outfit to replace the burlap sack the court had given him. They obtained several items made from a heavy, though moth-eaten and itchy wool: a pair of puffy legged pants, a heavy cloak, and a vest. They found a white shirt that fit Noah well enough, though it was stained with rust-colored spots. Finally, they secured some wool socks for the wooden shoes Noah had been issued. Noah still couldn't walk comfortably in them, in part because there was no right or left shoe. They were both the same, and it felt as if he were wearing two large canoes on his feet.

"Now you will be warm enough when we are out to sea," promised Jasper.

"Out to sea? I thought I was to help the master right here in New Amsterdam." Noah's breath caught in his chest.

"Did you now?" replied the amiable Jasper. "Well, we will be heading out to sea first thing tomorrow morning on the sixth of December, and you shall most assuredly be among us."

"It's too cold to be heading out to sea now!" Noah exclaimed desperately.

"Not for this master. We shall be sailing south, where the waters will soon be warmer," said Jasper jovially.

"You don't understand," Noah protested. "I have to stay in New Amsterdam."

"I don't think the master will approve of such a plan."

Noah looked down at the white shirt and trembled as he regarded what appeared to be bloodstains across its front. There had to be some way to avoid setting foot on that ship. If he left New Amsterdam, he knew he would never be able to find the Great Oak. As Noah buttoned up his new shirt, he tried not to imagine what might have happened to its previous owner. Why he wondered, did everything have to be so hard?

The following morning when Noah stepped out of the barn for the last time, he discovered that the world had been transformed. Everywhere, trees, houses, barns, stone fences, and wooden gates were covered in white. Noah fell in line behind Jasper who joined the parade of crew members making their way back to Fort Amsterdam. Above them, the padded quilt of sky dropped little bits of white onto their heads. With each step Noah took, his wooden clogs crunched into the white powder underfoot. He recalled the time he and his father, both wearing sneakers, stood in the thin layer of snow at the climate-controlled greenhouse. At the time, Noah believed that the simulated snowfall had given him a sense of what a real one had been like. But of course, it had not.

The world of the past now looked like an enchanted and magical place. As Noah looked out over the farmland, he remembered stories his mother had read to him when he was a little kid. Children's books about places long ago where *once upon a time there was snow.* In those stories, creatures large and small—field mice, hedgehogs, and bears—hiked through forests, sledded down hills, and built cozy forts in the ethereal white substance. The snow made Noah think about Eti. He remembered Eti telling him that its season was a beautiful one. Suddenly, Noah imagined hearing his voice.

"The river you travel on is long and winding. It is not yet time to give up," Eti's voice assured him.

The recently risen sun sat low on the horizon and sparkled the land, as the crew entered the village of New Amsterdam. They walked past small Dutch homes whose windows and doors were barred by wooden shutters against the bitter cold, protecting the sleeping families within.

"Have you forgotten what day it is?" Jasper asked excitedly as he turned to Noah.

Noah looked up at him, questioningly. While the other men continued walking, Jasper stopped in front of a small house and playfully put a finger up to his mouth to indicate that Noah should remain quiet. After all the crew members had passed, Jasper ran up to the house's door and retrieved a wooden shoe filled with treats: a sugared biscuit, a carved wooden doll, and a seashell. When a dog began to bark, Jasper took a peppercorn from his leather bag, placed the small spice in the shoe, and then quickly returned the shoe to its rightful spot.

"It is St. Nicholas' Day. Giving on this day always brings the giver good luck. We shall need all the luck we are granted as we set to sea in this bitter cold," he told Noah.

For the new settlers in the Northeastern colonies, the actual day of Christmas was a day of somber reflection. Yet New Amsterdam, unlike the other colonies, believed in having some fun and so they set aside a second day, St. Nicholas' Day, for doing so. The shoes had been filled with gifts for children. Later in the day, families would gather together to enjoy a great feast.

Noah continued trudging behind Jasper in his cumbersome clogs, for miles it seemed. They passed a windmill and a canal, which Jasper said had been built to give New Amsterdam the feeling of the old city back in Europe. When they arrived at the harbor, Noah looked around trying to find hints of the region that would exist in his future world. But he could not. The entire area was so different from the lower Manhattan Noah was familiar with. Aside from everything else, land that was underwater in Noah's world still bordered the harbor here.

Looking out across the bay, Noah spotted the *Engel*, whose name in English meant *Angel*, rocking gently back and forth over small waves. The tall sailing vessel, like the Mayflower, was a Dutch Cargo Fluyt. It reminded Noah of the *Galleon* pictured in one of his childhood books, *All About Ships*. Unlike a galleon, though, it was meant for the shipping trade and not for war.

The *Engel* was painted dark brown and red and had a square-shaped stern that was even steeper than the cliff Noah had jumped from while training with Taman by the lake. Two tall masts rose from its center, and a shorter one from its the stern. A fourth mast, called the bowsprit, stuck out from the bow and hung over the water. Though Noah would have loved to see the vessel under full sail, he dreaded the idea of boarding it.

If Noah had any hope of remaining in New Amsterdam, he would immediately have to inform Master Giles of his true purpose for being there. But he was not sure that was okay. When Eti had called him Noah, Eti had known exactly who Noah was. But the master had called him Noah in jest. Still, it was a risk Noah must take. Though he hoped the master would come to his senses and refuse to set sail in such cold weather, it didn't look like he was going to.

The snow flurries had stopped, but a biting wind blew in from the water and sliced through Noah's heavy wool coat. He looked out at the harbor where the two great rivers and the sea merged into one. As Eti had told him, one could feel the presence of the Great Spirit in this timeless place. Here, like the three great bodies of water, the past, present, and future seemed to flow into one another. Noah closed his eyes and stood silently as he asked the Great Spirit for guidance and strength.

A large wooden rowboat brought Noah, Jasper, and some of the other crew members out to the ship. After boarding the *Engel* by way of a treacherous rope ladder, the men rushed below deck to claim their sleeping berths. Jasper and the other men stored their meager possessions beneath their hammocks and then returned to the main deck. Noah remained below swaying on his bed—a heavy piece of canvas tied to the ship by a tangle of rope.

After gathering up his courage, Noah got up and walked through a narrow, low-ceilinged passageway to the poop cabin at the stern of the ship. He knocked hesitantly on a wooden door and waited until a voice inside commanded him to enter. Master Giles was sitting at a desk in the dark quarters, writing in a book by the light of an oil lamp. He looked up at Noah briefly and returned his gaze to his work.

"Why are you not on deck assisting the men?" the master asked, without looking back up.

"Sir, I came to New Amsterdam to find a tree," said Noah in the calm, soft voice that Joshua always recommended using when in trouble and who, unbeknownst to Noah, was now trying to use back in their world.

"A tree? And what type of tree would that be?" asked the master while continuing to scribble in his book.

"An oak tree known as the Grandmother Oak," said Noah, relieved by the master's seemingly calm demeanor.

"Ah! A quest for the great and mysterious oak."

"Do you know of this tree?" asked Noah.

"A charming fairy tale," the master answered dismissively as he dipped his pen nib into a pot of ink.

"Sir, the only reason I am here in your world is to find this tree that supposedly will help save the trees of my world," said Noah, trying to conceal his impatience.

"Your world, eh? And what world would that be?" retorted the master, as he looked up at Noah and fixed a steady gaze upon him.

"This world," whispered Noah, who withered under the master's glare.

"Well, that is reassuring." The master chuckled. "Tell, from whom did you hear of this tree? Pray it was not from Elizabeth. She is a true sorceress when it comes to spinning tales—and though that is part of her charm, she will surely get us both in great trouble one day."

"I didn't know you knew Elizabeth," said Noah.

"Why, Elizabeth is my truest friend and yours as well. It is she who assured me of your innocence. It is she who brought you to me. She saved your hide, my young friend."

"Why would I steal beaver pelts? Where I come from, killing an animal for fur or meat is illegal. What would we do with furs anyway? In my world, it's too warm to wear them."

"Your world! What is this nonsense?" demanded Master Giles.

"Sir, I'm begging you, I must remain in New York," Noah pleaded. "The tree is thought to live there, and I have to find it. The trees in my world are being killed off by a tree virus, and this tree may be their only hope."

"New York?" The master pounded his fist so hard on the table he nearly shattered his teacup. "I will hear no more of this outrageousness. Is it an oak tree you wish to find? You would be hanging from one if not for me."

Master Giles dismissed Noah and ordered him to return to the deck and mop it clear of water. Noah felt as if he were a small animal, caught in a fur hunter's snare. Back on deck, snow flurries, which had begun to fall once more, blew through the ship's riggings before disappearing into the slate blue sea. The crew raised the sails, and as they set out of the harbor Noah leaned out over the railing and watched helplessly as the distance between himself and the Great Island widened.

As the snow grew heavier and obscured the last view of New Amsterdam, Noah looked out at the icy ocean and wondered if he really would have been hung had the master not intervened. If so, then the man had saved his life and Noah should be grateful to him, not angry with him. Then Noah remembered Master Giles saying that Elizabeth too had saved his life. He recalled Elizabeth's appalling story of having been traded as an indentured slave. How different this world was from the one he called home.

Noah felt as if he were an alien visiting from another planet. The people here knew nothing about electricity or that microorganisms caused illness. For five months of the year, it was bitterly cold, and all anyone had for warmth were fireplaces, which only made their homes colder because all the heat escaped up through the chimney. And all that was just for starters. If only it had been possible for the world to have remained beautiful and clean, while at the same time progressing technologically and socially.

Noah filled with rage thinking about how the judge in New Amsterdam had readily and falsely accused him. The barbaric people of this world enslaved one another and hung one another for all kinds of stupid reasons. When several crew members walked past him, Noah couldn't help but glare at them.

"Are you feeling all right, lad? Has the sea sickness got into ye?" one of the crew members, who had seen the look on Noah's face, stopped to ask him. The man's voice was filled with compassion.

"No, I am fine," Noah answered, feeling ashamed of himself.

How could he lose himself so easily? Who was he to judge any of the people in this world anyway? They were the ancestors of all those who lived in his future time. Maybe they didn't know everything that their descendants knew. Development, after all, was a long process that extended across generations. Sometimes, as Ms. Rebecca had told them, terrible mistakes were made as part of that process.

Mistakes had indeed been made, and now Noah's world had arrived at a point where to continue it needed to backtrack and correct them, to reclaim what was lost and forgotten. As Noah thought about all this, he realized something else. He was a member of a species that had achieved, in a short period of time, what were arguably miracles. Perhaps he too was capable and had it in him to find a way to succeed.

While standing on the bow of the *Engel*, Noah felt the ship surging forward like a galloping horse. And as the boat reared up over the white-capped waves, he realized something. The ship's name sounded very much like the last name of the author, Madeleine L'Engle, who wrote his favorite childhood book.

# Chapter 21

For the next several mornings, Noah got up early and headed to the ship's forecastle where the kitchen was located. There, he assisted the cook with the preparation of breakfast. He then served tea to Master Giles in the steerage room, as the master manned the whip-staff, the wooden stick that controls the ship's rudder. After this was accomplished, Noah helped scrub the decks.

At night, Noah's dreams were as turbulent as the rolling sea. He would wake and calm himself by focusing on the sounds of the sleeping crew snoring all around him. A lack of appetite and a constitution that proved more seaworthy than expected, protected him from seasickness. Still, he felt miserable. In just two weeks, the winter solstice would arrive.

One night, almost a week after the ship's departure, Noah lay in his hammock unable to sleep. Quietly he got up, and being careful not to step on or disturb his bunkmates, left the closed sleeping quarters. Wrapped in a cloak and blanket, he climbed up the ladder to the deck and sat near the ship's bow under the star-filled sky. He was listening to a symphony of sounds—the muffled voices of the night crew, waves slapping against the boat's hull, the ship creaking as it strained forward, and a cold wind whistling through the sails—when an unfamiliar sound introduced itself. A mournful song rose up from the sea to the stars, where it seemed to echo off the vast dome of the sky.

"Humpbacks!" shouted one of the crew. "They are off the port side."

"What are they doing in these waters?" asked another.

"I do not know," replied the first.

Noah leaned as far as he could over the left side of the ship's bow and peered into the churning sea. He could not see the whales, though he heard them.

"Back away from there!" yelled a crew member, pulling Noah up by his collar. "No one will be diving in after ye should ye fall."

The men took lanterns and held them over the sides of the ship, lighting up a patch of ocean just off its bow.

"Sounds like there are a few of them, and they sound pretty close," said another of the crew.

A spout of water blasted in the circle of light, and the barely discernible shape of an enormous body surfaced and then disappeared into the darkness. One of the crew woke Master Giles, who quickly arrived on deck and sleepily assured everyone that the migrating whales would soon leave the area. Still, as a precautionary measure, the master ordered his men to lower the mainsail for the remainder of the night.

Noah felt sure that the whales were there because of him. He remained on deck, even after one of the high-ranking crew members ordered him to return to the crew's sleeping quarter. Fortunately, when the man went back to his duties, he forgot all about Noah. For the rest of the night, Noah remained on deck, tucked away behind a furled sail. Though he could no longer see the whales, he felt sure they were still there. In the morning, his belief was confirmed. The group of whales had remained and were now crossing the *Engel's* path as if they wanted to block her passage.

"I have never seen humpbacks try to interfere with a ship before," marveled one of the men.

Noah watched one of the large barnacle-encrusted mammals lift its body high out of the water on the ship's starboard side and crash down into the ocean. It was a jaw-dropping sight. A few drops of spray reached Noah, splashing the front of his coat. Master Giles, who had yet to make his decision on how to proceed, ordered his new apprentice, whom he observed standing idly on deck, to remember his morning chores.

"Master, I believe the whales are here to help me," Noah bravely asserted. "I've been trying to tell you that I have come back in time four hundred and fifty years just to find the Great Oak. I must bring one of her acorns back to my own time to save the trees of my world. The Great Oak lives somewhere near New Amsterdam, and I must return there and find her. I must do so before the winter solstice arrives."

Master Giles made no reply. He looked at Noah with a mixture of awe and anger.

"If there are only humpback whales, then maybe they are just migrating; but if a blue whale appears, then it is a sure sign you are being asked to bring me back to New Amsterdam," said Noah.

"Perhaps we shall toss you into the ocean and allow the whales to bring you back themselves," the master retorted.

"Please listen to me," Noah begged. "The trees of my world, the world of your descendants, are dying—and if they do, all of life may die with them."

"I have no children and therefore, no descendants," said the master before he turned and walked away. Noah then returned to his cabin in a state of despair and fell asleep.

By the next morning, frightening signs appeared that warned of an approaching storm. When Noah arrived on deck, he saw towering ocean swells and a brilliant red and pink sunrise that dazzled the eastern sky. Hanging on to the rigging as the deck slanted at steep angles, first up and then down, Noah looked for the humpback whales. They were still there, but they now blended into the ocean's hues, a steely slate blue traversed by the deep purple undersides of large, frightening swells. Every so often, a spout did appear and the crew, who now faced the threat of an approaching storm, seemed reassured by the whales' continued presence.

As the ship rose over the top of one enormous wave, Noah's eye caught a spout, about a quarter of a mile off of the starboard side, of a being just arriving. He watched in disbelief as a massive blue-gray body breached, dwarfing a passing swell, before slipping back into the water. Feeling sure of whom it was, Noah carefully made his way across the slippery, slanting deck in search of Master Giles. He found him at the bow of the ship, gazing at the turbulent ocean.

"Sir, she's here, like I said she would be. Please come see for yourself," relayed Noah, breathlessly.

"I am five days out on a rough winter sea. I cannot return to New Amsterdam without risk to this vessel and the entire crew whose lives depend on her." The ship's master did not look at Noah and seemed to be talking to himself.

As they stood there, the enormous leviathan rose up and nearly knocked into the bowsprit mast. Without a word, the master left Noah and quickly made his way to the ship's stern where he climbed to the poop deck.

"There is a storm ahead of us. The signs are many that we must change our course and postpone this voyage. Prepare to come about," the master addressed his crew. He then left the poop deck and returned to the steerage room.

While the master helmed the ship, a senior officer called out his commands to the crew.

"Ready about!" the officer yelled over the wind.

The crew all rushed to their stations, feverishly untying and pulling in long lengths of rope.

The whales, as if they knew what was happening, gave the *Engel* a wide berth as she moved forward.

When the ship was safely positioned between the ocean swells, the officer gave the second command.

"Hard alee!" he hollered.

Though a dangerous maneuver, the ship was turned into the wind. As the ship came about, the two sails that remained raised in the face of the storm ruffled furiously, until the *Engel's* bow pointed in the direction from which she had come.

For the rest of that day and all through the night, Master Giles remained in the steerage room, guiding the *Engel* safely over the stormy sea. The following morning when the sea had become calmer, he took a break and requested that the ship's newest apprentice bring him his breakfast. Quickly Noah raced from the deck, where he had been mopping up puddles of water, to fetch a tray of biscuits and tea to bring to the master's chamber. He found Master Giles sitting and contemplating an hourglass. After clearing some clutter from the desk, Noah placed the silver tray down. The master looked up and told him to sit in the seat across from him.

"Can you swim?" he asked, looking at Noah coldly.

"Yes, sir," replied Noah.

"Good then. Perhaps we shall let you swim to shore. Though it is a long way off and the water is frightfully cold."

Noah looked fearfully at the master and remained quiet.

"I've always felt it better to drown at sea than to hang in public," Master Giles continued.

For the first time on the voyage, Noah felt seasick. He looked down at his feet and held his head in his hands. Suddenly the master hammered his fist onto his desk, and Noah jumped up.

"I don't take kindly to the telling of falsehoods!" the master yelled.

"I have been telling you the truth," Noah yelled back. "I live on this same planet called Earth, but have come back in time from the year 2084."

"Pray tell, does Elizabeth know of your strange tale? That lovely and honest creature took pity on you and believed you to be innocent."

"No, she does not," answered Noah. "When I arrived in this world, a man named Taman greeted me and told me of my mission. He said that I must only reveal my identity to those who address me by name. You had called me Noah."

"Did I? Ah, yes, I did," the master mused.

Noah waited fearfully as he watched the master turn the hourglass in his hand. They remained silent while the steady stream of sand filled the hour glass's lower beaker.

"If only time could be controlled in such a manner. We travel too quickly into the future," mused Master Giles, briefly changing the subject.

"You say you have traveled back in time from the year 2084. You have come a long way back," the master noted dryly. "I have no reason to doubt your tale, but it is the West India Trading Company whom you must convince. I have no choice but to deliver you to them once we make land."

"You cannot do that, sir. They are crazy!" Noah had jumped out of his chair.

"My hide is already in peril. By aborting this voyage, I have put the Southern Settlements at risk by depriving them of needed provisions. Should I commit further treason by abetting a runaway felon, for whom I have assumed guardianship? Then my fate will be sealed."

"And if you turn me in to that company, all hope will be lost not just for me, but for the world of the future."

Master Giles leaned back in his chair and looked at Noah intently.

"I will consider your request for leniency. Now be off with you," the master sighed.

"At the very least, sir, please promise me you won't tell anyone what I have told you."

"You can be sure I will not be discussing any of this with a soul. I will let you know how I decide this matter."

Just after Noah left the master's chambers, someone on deck yelled. "Rogue wave off the port side!"

The ship slanted so steeply that Noah slid across the floorboards and fell against a wall. He clung to a wooden bench that was nailed to the floor as the ship then tilted in the opposite direction.

"Man overboard, man overboard!" someone yelled from above.

Master Giles burst through his office door and bounded up the ladder leading to the deck.

"A false alarm!" another hollered in return. "It's only the coat belonging to that young scoundrel that sailed off the bow of its own accord."

In his haste to see the master, Noah had forgotten about his coat. He had taken it off while mopping so as not to drench it in water. When he next looked up, he saw that the master had returned. The man stood at the top of the stairwell, looking down at him with a glint in his eye.

"A drowned man need not fear pursuit," said the master, as he sauntered down the ladder. "Quickly now, return to my cabin. You are to remain there until further notice."

Noah thought he understood what Master Giles had in mind. It would be a risky play to stage, yet there didn't seem to be any better one.

# Chapter 22

The *Engel's* crew was informed that the young thief was indeed missing, and it became assumed by all that it wasn't only a coat that had fallen overboard. After a few more days out on the rough open sea, the ship sailed safely past Nut Island, into the bay of New Amsterdam, and dropped anchor on the morning of December 17. Noah remained hidden in the master's quarters on board the *Engel*, while the rest of the ship's crew was ferried ashore.

After the crew returned to the barracks where they had previously stayed, Jasper, along with William, another of the master's trusted crew members, returned to the ship under the cover of night to retrieve Noah. The two men rowed across the bay in a sea as still and smooth as glass, quite different from what it had been just a few days before. As he had done when rescued by Eti, Noah crouched down and hid in the bottom of their small craft. When they arrived on land, Jasper and William tucked Noah into the back of a horse-drawn cart and brought him to the small farm where Elizabeth worked.

Elizabeth's employers were away for the Christmas holiday. She was alone at the farm, while they were visiting relatives in one of the new colonies north of New Amsterdam. When the men knocked on the door, Elizabeth cautiously opened its top half and examined them as they explained the purpose of their late-night visit. Though hesitant, she allowed them to enter the home. Upon hearing that Master James Giles had requested it of her, she readily agreed to offer shelter to Noah. She seemed quite happy and relieved to learn that the master was well and had come back to New Amsterdam. While the men warmed themselves by the fire, Elizabeth asked them many questions about their voyage and the master's meeting with officials.

"The master told of many signs warning of disaster. He told of the sea rising higher than the tallest trees in New Amsterdam, of ominous clouds appearing at sunrise, and of a strange gathering of whales blocking the ship's passage," Jasper relayed to Elizabeth as she listened intently.

"Was it all true?" she asked.

Jasper nodded and then looked sheepishly at both Noah and William.

"The master also told of the loss of the young thief, who had been whale-gazing on deck when a wave knocked him overboard," William spoke honestly.

"And yet here he sits. Did any suspect the master of having borne a false witness?" worried Elizabeth.

"Not of yet, ma'am," said William.

"Was the master's testimony well received?" asked Elizabeth.

"The officials felt the turnabout was in good judgment," said Jasper. "As to the loss of our thief, only one expressed an opinion. The gentleman felt such a demise was too poetic for one so lowly."

With a mischievous grin on his face, Jasper gestured toward an appalled Noah.

"The master's instructions are that the boy remain here until he gives word that it is safe for him to depart. The master will contact you soon, Miss," said the more reserved William.

"Thank you!" said Elizabeth. She gave them each a slice of bread with some cheese as they readied to leave.

"Soon you will be able to return to the mountains and the home of your aunt and uncle. Travel safely and be well. May we meet again one day," Jasper said to Noah. He tipped his hat and bowed lightly to Elizabeth, before he and William stepped out into the cold night.

Elizabeth set Noah up in the small, cave-like alcove under the eaves of the roof that served as her bedroom. A narrow passageway connected it to the children's nursery on the other side of the attic, where Elizabeth would stay while Noah remained in the house. Though no more than a crawl space, Elizabeth had turned her alcove into a charming nest. Dried herbs and flowers from the previous summer hung from rough and splintering wooden beams, as did a small lantern. A basket full of seashells and a ceramic bowl full of water sat on a wooden bench by a wall. There was a small braided rug covering the unfinished floor and a painting of a ship nailed to the only wall not slanted by the roof.

Noah curled up in the feather bed and quilt that covered a sleeping pallet. He was thankful for both, as the house's attic was as drafty and cold as any of the other lodgings he had stayed in while in New Amsterdam. As his body warmed the bed, he watched the lantern's candlelight dance on the ceiling beams overhead. While at present he felt secure and content, Noah knew that he wouldn't truly be safe until he had found the tree.

Though he'd agreed to wait for the master's approval before setting off, Noah was now anxious to be on his way. The winter solstice would arrive in just a few days. Still, he could not risk either his own or the master's safety. If he were discovered walking about New Amsterdam, both their lives would be in jeopardy. Perhaps even now it was too late to find the Great Oak. Still, Noah must try and not allow himself to consider the possibility of failure.

On the second evening of Noah's stay with Elizabeth, a hard knock on the door startled them both. When Elizabeth asked for their visitor's identity, they were both elated to hear Master James Giles' voice. They opened the door and found him standing at the its threshold, smiling and in high spirits. He had brought with him what looked to be a hamper of food and two wrapped parcels, one much larger than the other.

The master stamped snow from his boots and brought the packages into the firelit house. With a broad smile, he unpacked smoked sturgeon, bean soup, bread, cheese, and a jug of beer from the hamper. He then presented the larger of the two parcels to Noah. After tearing his package open, Noah regarded the contents in disbelief.

"But how were you able to?" he asked incredulously.

"The seas we encountered foretold of a terrible storm which fast approaches. Such was confirmed by the master of a ship named the *Constance*, who arrived at port soon after the *Engel*. The company was ever so grateful to me for having averted a disaster."

Noah's parcel contained all the things that the court of New Amsterdam had taken from him. Inside were his deerskin clothes and pack, his boots, mittens, hat, and the mantle Ro had made from raccoon and beaver skins. His leather pouch still contained the wampum beads she had put there.

"I asked the judge for the belongings of my crew member lost at sea. In the spirit of Christmas, he returned them, requesting that I deliver them to his next of kin. I suppose you will suffice as next of kin."

"Thank you," Noah managed to say.

"This is a gift for the lady of this house," the master's eyes twinkled as he handed Elizabeth the smaller package.

Elizabeth untied the paper parcel. Inside was a large rectangular table scarf whose intricate pattern looked to be made from the same snowflakes whose beauty Eti had attested to. As Elizabeth held up the white linen cloth, its lacy shadow danced on the wall opposite the fire.

"Mind, that one is not for you. It is for the owners of this house to whom I will be asking for your hand in marriage. There is another one just like it waiting by for you," said the master, smiling gently.

Elizabeth carefully rewrapped the table scarf and as her eyes filled with tears, she looked up at the master and smiled back.

The master then turned to Noah. "My young friend, I ask that you dine with us and wait until morning to depart. Though none will come searching for you, many of my crew are out and about, celebrating. By morning most shall be asleep. Then, the only trouble I fear you may encounter is a storm. Though we averted her at sea, she may reach us yet. There is no telling of this."

"Master, after the new year, please tell Elizabeth all I have told you," Noah requested.

"I will be sure and do just that," promised Master Giles. "I wish you Godspeed on your journey and will hold you in my prayers and heart."

At the start of the new year, Elizabeth's guardians would approve of the master's proposal, and the couple would marry in the early spring just as the trees had begun to flower. Soon after, they would take one more voyage on the *Engel*, bringing the long overdue supplies to the Southern Settlements. Upon their return, the master would resign from his post at the West India Trading Company and with his meager savings, purchase farmland in the river valley of New Netherland. There, he and Elizabeth would raise a large family and build a small brewery that would one day become one of the region's finest. All of this and much more would happen in the future, but on the present evening, the couple sat together with Noah in the main room of the little farmhouse, listening to the cold, whistling wind while eating their dinner by the fire.

# Chapter 23

Noah spent most of his last night in New Amsterdam lying awake and worrying. He remembered Taman saying that the Great Oak would be found only by one it chooses. What if he were no longer worthy of that honor because of the mistakes he'd made and the lies he'd told?

Early in the morning, after he had finally fallen asleep, the sound of a loud banging woke him. The shutters on the hallway window had opened and were knocking against the window's frame. An icy wind blew in, and the attic became even colder than it had been. Getting out of his warm bed, Noah walked over to the window to close it. Outside, a squirrel peered in at him from the window's ledge. The small creature looked like she wanted to come into the house. Perhaps she was seeking shelter for her family.

"It's not much warmer in here than it is out there," Noah whispered to her.

Upon hearing Noah speak, the squirrel dashed away.

Returning to his bed, Noah looked about Elizabeth's room. When he first saw it, he thought Elizabeth's employers were selfish for having given her only an attic crawl space to sleep in within their home. The alcove had seemed better suited to a squirrel, such as the one he'd just seen. But after spending his first night in it, he changed his mind and now felt it was as cozy a nest as anyone could ask for. It had provided him with warmth and security and he dreaded leaving it. Yet he knew that to remain any longer was dangerous. Getting out of the warm bed once more, he shivered as he prepared for the last part of his journey.

In the predawn darkness, Noah wrapped himself in his fur mantle and collected his belongings. He then tiptoed through the narrow passageway to the staircase by the nursery. Though he tried to remain quiet, it was impossible. Even the lightest step yielded a loud creak from the wide floorboards. The narrow staircase was just as noisy, and when Noah reached the house's first floor, certain that he had not awakened Elizabeth, he was greatly relieved.

In the main room, all that remained of the blazing fire from the night before were a few glowing embers. Noah sat down at the small table, and by the dim light began to write a note to Elizabeth. He had no idea if she could even read. Dipping the quill pen into a pot of ink, he drew on a piece of parchment paper, a simple stick figure with one hand placed on its heart and the other pointing to a tree. Beneath this drawing he wrote:

Dear Elizabeth,

    I came to New Amsterdam to find a tree known as The Great Oak. Master Giles told me that you know all about this tree. He promised that he would tell you about me after I left. I want to thank you and the master for everything you've done for me.

Very Truly Yours,
Noah Bradbury

After leaving the note on the table, Noah found the cheese and bread left over from dinner and packed them into his leather bag. He then released the latch to the front door and stepped through it, leaving behind the security of the small Dutch home. Outside, a few bright stars, aided by the waning moon, cast a dim light that reflected off the remaining snow, allowing for some visibility on this second longest night of the year.

Noah was about to set off when the tall, lanky figure of a man emerged from the pale-yellow doorway of a neighboring building. Quickly, Noah slipped behind a corner of the house and waited for the man to leave. He thought most of New Amsterdam would still be asleep, but now realized that nighttime revelers and early rising farmers might be up and about. He would have to be careful. When the man disappeared on the road leading into town, Noah stepped out from hiding.

Walking back to the front of the house, Noah scanned the landscape. He had no idea how or where to even begin searching for the Great Oak. He was looking up at the sky, hoping for some divine inspiration, when a loud chattering interrupted the night's stillness. A squirrel had run into the middle of the road that passed in front of the house. The small creature, possibly the same one who had been on the window ledge, was standing on her hind legs looking directly at Noah, sounding as if she were scolding him.

Recalling how Taman had told him his guides would be animals as well as people, Noah began to walk toward her. The jittery rodent seemed frightened by this and immediately ran up the road, away from him. But when a comfortable distance had been reached between them, the squirrel stopped and looked back at Noah. Though unsure about doing so, Noah's instincts told him to continue to follow her. Together they began to walk in a northeasterly direction away from New Amsterdam.

Noah remained several paces behind his would-be guide who continued to stop, look back, and chatter at him. In the bitter predawn cold, they passed New Amsterdam's outermost farms and shack-like homes until they reached a stone fence that delineated the town's boundary. The squirrel scampered up and over the piled granite rocks and Noah, who had begun to doubt his instincts, reluctantly did so as well.

Leaving the comfort of the road, the squirrel darted onto a vast snow-covered field where farmers would bring their sheep to graze in the spring. She led Noah toward a forest on its far side that bordered the eastern river. The sun was now rising behind a low-lying bank of clouds, streaking the horizon with deep reds and purples, making the surrounding landscape more visible. This meant that Noah too could now be seen. Quickly, he made his way across the field over the thin layer of crusty snow, toward the relative security of the trees.

The area by the edge of the forest was dotted with tree stumps. It looked like loggers had been cutting down trees for all the new construction being built in New Amsterdam. A majestic hemlock that could have been the template for the fake one in the museum, had been left standing, tall and proud, nearby. Noah figured that it too would soon be cut down. He wished he could return to New Amsterdam just for a moment and tell its residents how priceless and irreplaceable their trees were. But that was impossible and besides, he doubted they would listen to him.

Being careful of his ankle, Noah shuffled into the woods after the squirrel on what looked to be an old trail. It led to a frozen stream where Noah sat down on a log to rest. There, the voice of a bird broke the surrounding stillness, and Noah looked up to see a fiery, red snippet careening overhead. Noah recognized the showy male cardinal from having seen his picture in one of his mother's cherished ornithology books. The red cardinal flew onto the branch of a hickory tree, and when Noah walked over to admire him, the squirrel chattered harshly. The small creature seemed to be reminding Noah not to get distracted.

They hiked more deeply into the woods along the now hard-to-discern trail. The trees here were much larger than the ones at the forest's periphery. As they walked among these old beings, Noah felt their powerful yet serene presence. He had stopped to admire an old elm tree when the red cardinal flew passed him. Noah watched the tiny red speck fly ahead and disappear into a tree that he had not even noticed. The tree was a giant who seemed to stand alone, even among those who surrounded it like immediate family members.

Timidly, Noah walked up to the ancient being whose uppermost branches were bathed in a halo of light. It appeared as if the rising sun held the tree in its favor. The tree's vast canopy of branches spread out over the tops of the other trees as if to protect them, leaving the ground beneath mostly free of snow. As Noah walked over a springy moss that carpeted the ground, he spotted the squirrel sitting on one of the tree's lower branches, contentedly nibbling an acorn. Cautiously, Noah reached out and gently put his hand on the tree's massive trunk. Its coarse bark was wrinkled and cracked like the skin of a beloved elder.

"The tree will only be found by one it chooses," he heard Taman say.

Sitting down on the moss, Noah craned his neck back and looked up at the tree's lattice of branches that still bore a few of the green leaves of summer. The branches partitioned the sky, framing it into sections, each one a unique shape, patterned with dots and streaks in cerulean blue, lavender, and salmon pink. When Noah's neck began to ache, he lay down on his back and continued looking up at the sunrise-filled patches of sky until he fell asleep.

He slept through the morning until noontime. When he awoke, he saw that the cloud bank that had been on the horizon earlier had moved in overhead. Groggily, Noah stood up. Just as he noticed the dancing snow flurries that had begun to fall, something else more solid and substantial dropped to the earth beside him. It was a single acorn attached to a small green leaf. Noah picked up the acorn and looked up at the tree.

"Thank you," he whispered as his eyes filled with tears.

He stood still and held the acorn, before gently putting it into the leather pouch about his neck.

"Thank you!" Noah hollered out to the squirrel, but both she and the red cardinal were nowhere to be seen.

Now alone, Noah realized there was little time to spare. Though it seemed impossible, he had to try to get back to the portal at Stissing Mountain by midnight. He retraced his steps along the trail through the woods, past the pond and back toward the field that he and the squirrel had crossed earlier that morning. He decided he would return to the outskirts of New Amsterdam and find the road that might one day be Broadway, upon which he'd arrived. Maybe this time he would meet a friendlier farmer who would offer him a ride to the top of the island. Once there, if he could find a way to cross the river, he would just have to continue traveling north and east.

By the time Noah reached the field, the pretty snow flurries had turned into a frozen rain, and a gnawing hunger filled his stomach. Noah took the bread and cheese the master had brought him and Elizabeth the night before out from his pack. While he ate, the icy pellets made soft clinking sounds like minuscule pieces of glass as they hit the crusty snow on the ground around him. At the edge of the field, a small group of pine trees offered shelter, but Noah refused to stop. Instead, he forced himself to keep trudging on through the cold and dreary landscape.

The thick white blanket of cloud overhead had deleted all the morning's color, muting the landscape into a pale blue gray. This allowed Noah to immediately see the flash of red that appeared at the opposite end of the field. Squinting at what he thought might be the red cardinal, he saw instead a fox standing among the trees. Noah was sure it was the same animal he'd seen weeks ago. Frantically he began waving his arms.

"I am here!" Noah shouted. "Please help me get back to the diorama!"

# Chapter 24

The small fox waited for Noah to cross the field and then began to lead him—not in the direction back toward New Amsterdam but on a northern route away from it. They hiked through the woods, past a dismal settlement of small shacks, while the icy rain continued to fall. Noah tucked his chin into the warmth of his fur mantle, trying not to worry about the possibility that the storm the master had warned of was arriving. Instead, he focused on following the fox, entrusting his life to the small red-coated animal.

As they walked, the frozen rain turned back into snow. Noah stopped to gaze at a farmhouse whose chimney billowed smoke into the now flurry-filled air. He stood still, imagining a big copper pot of bread and beer porridge heating over the blazing fire within. He had not liked that porridge, yet he would welcome a steaming bowl of it now, as he warmed himself by the farmhouse's fireplace. When the fox began to whine and snarl,

Noah regained his senses and resumed walking. It was as if an invisible leash connected them, though it was the fox who was in its control.

Noah was quite sure it was not possible to reach Stissing Mountain by midnight. Still, he had faith that his guide would lead him to safety. While they hiked, the woods became still and peaceful as the powdery snow fell. Noah was walking in a meditative rhythm several yards behind his guide when the quiet was shattered by the bark of an unseen hound. Taking cover behind a birch tree, Noah looked back in the direction from which it had come. He scanned the entire area, but there was nothing to be seen except trees and snow.

"A drowned man need not fear pursuit," Noah remembered the master saying.

But what if it was discovered that Noah had not really drowned? Was it possible there were people out searching for him? Noah reasoned that the bark most likely belonged to a farm dog. Still, he felt afraid. Stepping out from behind the birch tree, he walked quickly toward the fox who had fearlessly continued leaping through the snow and now waited at the edge of another large open field. Looking at the red-coated animal, Noah realized that his guide had as much to fear as he did.

Noah had almost reached the field when a soft voice behind him ordered him to halt. When he turned around, he saw a man and a boy standing with their hound several yards away. The man, dressed in a black cloak, had a pack hanging over his shoulder and what looked to be a logger's ax swinging by his side. Noah saw that the boy carried a rabbit on his back and wore a fur mantle identical to the one Taman had given him.

"Is this he?" asked the man. Neither the man nor the boy showed any interest in the fox.

"It is!" the boy nodded.

Noah looked at the young thief closely. When he'd last encountered him, he had assumed the boy didn't understand English, but apparently he did.

"He is your fur thief! He stole that mantle from me, as well as the beaver skin pelts from the West India Trading Company!" Noah yelled.

"I do not care who stole the furs. I care only for the bounty I shall receive upon delivering you to the court. The court officials shall determine your guilt or innocence, as they will that of your master's," sneered the man.

The man bound Noah's wrists together in front of Noah's chest. Then, taking hold of Noah's arm, the man began to drag him back into the woods, away from the field where the fox waited. Noah fought to resist, but the hound growled and nipped at his ankles.

"Get a move on, son," ordered the man. "If not, I shall tie you to a tree and retrieve you in the morning. Be you dead or alive, I will collect my reward."

As the sun began its early descent, the bounty hunter, seemingly in a hurry to reach shelter, quickened his pace and pulled Noah firmly along toward New Amsterdam. They walked in silence, while the snow began to fall more heavily. From behind them, embedded within the rising voice of the wind, Noah thought he heard the fox's impatient whine. When he turned to look back for his faithful companion, his captor pulled him roughly forward. But just before he did, Noah caught a glimpse of another much larger being.

"Keep pace!" the man threatened. He tightened his grip on Noah's wrists so firmly that it was sure to leave an angry bruise.

But Noah was now more frightened by what he had just seen than he was of the man. The man dragged him along for another fifty yards, when up ahead they saw that the hound and fur thief had come to a stop. There, standing in their path, was a brown and black-coated wolf. This canine looked smaller than the one Noah had seen. Still, the creature was no less frightening. The wolf began to whine and walk slowly toward the hound and the fur thief. Then in a sudden and unexpected move, the animal leapt at the hound and grabbed her by her neck.

"Leave her be!" the man bellowed, unfastening his ax.

Just then, the whine Noah had heard earlier sounded again, this time more clearly, from behind them. Noah turned to see the much larger wolf now approaching. The fur thief, showing no concern for either his older companion or the hound, ran off into the blowing and swirling snow, abandoning them both.

"Get thee back!" the man hollered, but the agile young thief was now too far away to hear him.

Wrapping an arm about Noah's chest and using him as a shield, the man brandished his ax. Slowly, he backed away from the wolves, pulling Noah along with him. When he had reached a comfortable distance, he pushed Noah to the ground as if making the wolves an offering. Then he too scurried away, chasing the quickly vanishing trail of footprints left by his cowardly accomplice.

After the man's departure, the smaller wolf released the hound and walked to the side of the larger one. They stared at Noah and the hound, while the snow fell around them, clinging to their thick coats. Together, they looked like a male and female, perhaps a mating couple.

The two wolves remained only briefly, before they too disappeared into the blurry vision of trees. After their departure, Noah, with his hands still bound, managed to stand up. He looked over at the now docile hound. She appeared unharmed, though she looked back at Noah through round watery eyes that seemed frightened and confused. The poor dog barked twice, before running after her unfaithful masters in the direction of New Amsterdam.

Now alone, Noah looked around at the woods. He recognized some of the trees that he and the fox had passed earlier. Based on their presence, Noah guessed the men had taken him about a half a mile away from the field. That was a distance he and his friends regularly sprinted. Still, in what now appeared to be a mounting storm—with bound hands and an ankle that he still had to be careful of—that same distance would be much harder to cover. The unseen sun was about to set and when it did, it would leave the world in complete darkness. Noah had to reach the white expanse of field while there was still light enough to see by. He only hoped the fox had waited for him.

Noah's bound hands made it hard for him to keep his balance and he continually fell in the deepening snow. Still, he pressed on. As he pushed against the storm, he lowered his head to shield his face from the stinging, wind-driven flakes. His eyes and nose would not stop running and he kept having to wipe them with the mittens on his tied hands. But by staying close to the trees, using them as guides and for support, he was able to make his way back to the field before nightfall.

When he arrived at the field's edge, he spotted a red tail bopping in the sea of white and purple shadows. The fox had waited for him.

"I'm here!" Noah called out.

The fox looked back at him before standing up and shaking himself off. He then began leaping in and out of the snow in the same manner that the whales had in the ocean. Following him onto the field, Noah bent over and pushed forward against the wind. Every breath he took of the cold air felt painful as it entered his lungs.

The snow had been blown unevenly across the field's terrain, and in some areas Noah stepped into a depth that reached up to his thighs. He tried to remain at higher elevations, where the tips of grass and shrubs were still visible, but when he reached the center of the field, he stumbled into a pocket of snow so deep that he was unable to get back up. He sat in fear, looking around at the perimeter of the field as the landscape darkened.

Exercise had kept Noah warm, but now that he stopped moving, the kind of cold he'd felt while submerged in the river began to engulf him once more. Pushing himself onto his knees, he tried to climb out of the snow, but he was just too weak. The fox had reached the other end of the field and had climbed up to a ridge where the woods began again. His yellow eyes looked piercingly back at Noah.

"How could Eti ever have thought I would like this stuff?" Noah asked himself as he closed his eyes.

He envisioned his warm world and wondered why he would want to inflict any of this upon it. Maybe it was for the best that the acorn remain in the past. A wolf, or was it the wind's howl, prompted him to look up once more. Standing on the ridge, the fox was now staring at a point on the other side of the field. Noah turned to see a circle of light heading toward him across the darkening landscape. In the light's center, he made out a figure clothed in the furs of a hunter who moved with the agility of a young man.

Not wolves, nor even a storm, would deter that fur thief. Beneath his fur mantle, Noah felt Ro's pouch rise and fall against his chest with each breath. He felt a renewed determination to protect the small treasure it held, no matter the cost. But as the figure drew near, Noah discovered that it was not the fur thief, but a young man he had never seen before.

Noah saw that the young man wore what looked like two tennis rackets on his feet. He carried a second pair of rackets on his back and walked with the help of two wooden poles, one of which bore a lantern in whose light the snow blew furiously.

"You are almost there," the figure called out to him over the screeching wind.

When the young man arrived, he knelt down beside Noah and cut the rope off his wrists. He then gave Noah a flask of water to drink from and a piece of bread, before tossing the rackets on his back, to the ground. After strapping them to Noah's feet, he helped Noah stand up. The snowshoes allowed Noah to remain on the surface of the snow.

"My name is Elan. I am Taman's son. The portal you will return home by is a mile away!" he shouted over the wind.

"Okay!" was the only reply Noah could manage.

Using one of Elan's walking poles, Noah began following him across the remainder of the field. Rather than heading directly into the wind, they walked at an angle to it, tacking back and forth toward their destination, the way the *Engel* had on the ocean. Darkness had settled over the land and if not for Elan's lantern they would be unable to see. Noah tried to locate the yellow-eyed fox, but he could not find him anywhere. He hoped the animal had returned to a warm and safe home.

When they reached the hill, they climbed up it sideways. At its top, they took their snowshoes off and sat down on the tree-lined ridge to rest. The wind died down and the heavy snowfall stopped. Taking off his boots, Noah emptied them of snow and tried to warm his toes in his hands.

Has the storm passed?" he asked.

"The storm too is taking a rest. It will grow strong again. That is why we must hurry," Elan told him.

"I cannot feel my feet," said Noah.

"They will heal once you are home. My father told me to tell you he is proud of you," Elan encouraged him.

In the light of the lantern, Noah followed Elan's tracks as they moved forward along the higher elevation. The snowshoes strapped to his feet lifted up and sank back down, one after the other, as if they had a will of their own. When they reached the end of the ridge, they carefully descended sideways down a steep slope that led to a small clearing. There, Elan planted his pole, from which the lantern hung, into the snow.

"We shall find the portal here," he announced.

"When I arrived here, the portal was a cave," Noah replied, bending over to breathe.

Elan walked to the center of the clearing, knelt down, and dug through the snow with his mittens. He uncovered the icy surface of a small pond.

"This is a different portal," Elan affirmed. "Look through the ice and you shall see."

Noah took off his snowshoes and joined Elan on the pond. He sat down and peered into the ice. There was a dim light coming up from the pond's murky depths, and within it Noah saw the shadowy images of two people walking.

"You must break through the ice and travel back," Elan said looking steadily at Noah. "This is the last thing you have to do. Soon you will be home."

"I cannot do that. There has to be another way," said Noah, as he quickly walked off the pond.

"It is the only way, Noah," said Elan. "Your friend Tessa is here. She has been collecting many seeds. If the acorn takes root, she will be able to bring the seeds back to your world. If not, she will return to your world without them. She will leave here on the summer solstice and arrive on the day this future land will celebrate its independence."

"So, Tessa is here. I thought she might be," Noah said, trying to breathe.

"She is fine. You must hurry, Noah," said Elan.

"Please make sure she is safe," Noah said to the young man before him, trying to conceal a new feeling of jealousy.

"She is safe," Elan replied.

"If I dive into that pond I will drown." Noah thought how ironic it was that the master had reported him as being drowned to the authorities back in New Amsterdam. At least now, no one would be able to call the master a liar.

"Within this pond we can see people walking. This pond is a portal, and you will not drown. You will travel through it and arrive in your own time," assured Elan.

"What about you?" Noah worried for Elan's safety, despite his feeling of rivalry.

"There is a farm nearby where I may take shelter," assured Elan.

On the ridge above, two yellow eyes appeared out of the darkness and looked down into Noah's own.

"I hope we will meet again, Noah. Go now in peace and safety," said Elan.

Noah heard the wolf panting but could not see him. When the fearsome canine walked down from the ridge, Noah recognized him in the lantern light. Neither of the two wolves he had seen earlier had been him.

"He is a friend," Noah remembered Taman telling him, as the animal who had chased him in the museum threatened him once more.

Noah backed onto the pond. His eyes were focused only on the wolf's own when the ice beneath him cracked. He slipped and fell, and as he struggled to stand up, the ice gave way completely. The cold water pierced every nerve ending and knocked the wind from his chest, rendering him incapable of breathing. It happened so quickly there was no time to object or feel afraid. Beyond the blue and white he fell, to a place where there was no cold at all, where a light awaited him.

## Chapter 25

Joanne Bradbury had told her husband, Matthew, all about the dream she'd had during their stay at the museum.

"I think the note I found was asking us to return to the museum on New Year's Eve," she informed him.

Initially, Matthew had agreed to spend the New Year at the museum. But when the media and politicians began issuing unrelenting reports of a colossal hurricane that was expected to make landfall in New York at that time, he changed his mind.

"Joanne, I don't think it's reasonable for us to risk our lives because of a dream you've had," he argued. "We can go to the museum immediately after the storm passes."

But Joanne did not want to wait. After a sleepless night on December 31, she decided that she would go to the museum on her own. She packed some food and clean clothes for herself and Noah and took the office key that her husband's colleague had given them. She knew her husband would be upset with her, but that he and their daughter would be fine. Later in the day they, along with her parents, would enter the institute's underground shelter where they were sure to remain safe. After writing a quick note to Matthew who was still asleep, she quietly left the apartment.

It was dark outside, but Joanne was happy she'd gotten an early start. Not only had it allowed her to avoid a confrontation with her husband, but it meant she would be able to get on a train. The news reported that service to and from the city would stop by midmorning. As Joanne walked to the bus depot, past path lights that shimmered in the steamy fog, she felt as if she were traveling under water. Everywhere, the palm trees had been stripped of their holiday lights and decorations in preparation for the storm. Though the institute's grounds now looked dismal, this was fine with Joanne. She was grateful that this horrible holiday season was almost over.

The bus left the depot and quickly arrived at the train station. Once she boarded a train, Joanne felt a sense of relief. It was practically empty, and she found a seat by herself next to a window. As the train sped toward the city, she watched hypnotically as droplets of rain moved like snails across the window's glass, leaving streaky trails behind them. The train's motion lulled her to sleep, and she did not wake until it reached a security checkpoint where military officials asked for everyone's identification.

Joanne had to provide her identification to officials two more times—when she boarded the city's subway system and again at the museum, where she handed over her clearance form to the head of security. She worked hard to convince the man, whom someone had called Russell that she had good reason to believe her missing son might return that evening from wherever he had been.

"I really shouldn't admit you, ma'am, but after what you have gone through, I'm not going to turn you away," he said, waving her inside.

Joanne immediately rode the elevator up to her husband's colleague's office. There, she worked on editing her doctoral dissertation until the early afternoon, when the arriving storm made it hard for her to concentrate. Not wanting to be alone any longer, she walked down to the museum's main entrance where the security team had set up their station. She joined the group of people who were sitting at a long table, drinking coffee and listening to public radio while playing cards and chess. Through the glass doorway, she could see sheets of rain pouring down, while the trees, sweet gum and eucalyptus, swayed wildly as they struggled to maintain their hold on the earth.

"What in the name—!" Russell had suddenly jumped up, startling everyone.

He ran to the front entrance where just outside the glass doors a drenched figure cowered, protecting itself, as a small animal might from being blown away.

Joanne stood up, unable to breathe, as Russell and another guard struggled to open the door. She was sure it was Noah, but when the guards pulled in a drenched and bedraggled Joshua, she stared in disbelief.

"I ought to have you sent to juvenile court. Sit right there and don't move," Russell barked, pointing to a chair.

Joshua sat down in the chair and looking intently at the floor, tried to avoid making eye contact with anyone.

Joanne regarded him with a mixture of resentment and disappointment, until the puddle forming beneath his chair brought her back to her senses.

"I have Noah's clothes with me. Can I bring him to the office so he can change into them?" she asked Russell.

"Ma'am, I understand what you are going through, and I made an allowance for you to be here—but this boy?"

"You can't send him home now, Russell," another guard interjected.

"I understand that," Russell barked. "Fine, go get him into some dry clothes."

In silence, Joanne walked with Joshua to a bank of elevators where she inserted her security key into the card reader on the wall.

"Does your mother know you are here?" she asked, without looking at him.

"No!" replied Joshua, looking down at the floor.

"Won't she be worried?" Joanne turned to him after they boarded an elevator.

"I told her I would be at my new school's shelter. She and my brother are staying with my grandmother at her shelter," he answered.

"So why are you here?" Joanne asked as she unlocked the office door. Once inside, she handed him Noah's clean pants and a T-shirt.

"In a dream, I found a note that told me to be here," he replied.

Joanne was taken aback. "I did too," she said softly. "We shall see if our dreams mean anything."

Before returning to the main entrance, Joanne found books for both her and Joshua. For the rest of the afternoon, they both tried to sit and read while outside the mounting wind shrieked like some furious and vengeful spirit.

At dinnertime, one of the guards placed a platter of protein meats, a large bowl of pasta, and some bread on the table, though no one had much of an appetite. Later, plates of cookies and a drink resembling old-fashioned eggnog were brought out. For the remainder of 2084, the gathered group listened to the beautiful holiday symphony being broadcast on the radio, while trying to shut out the horrifying wind that backed it up outside. Just before midnight, a terrible explosion sounded from somewhere in the city. The lights began to blink on and off, and the radio stopped playing Handel's Messiah.

"Well, I guess that means it's time for the midnight rounds," quipped Russell, who had been enjoying the symphony. "Who wants to join me?"

"Sounds like a power station just went out. I'll join you. I think it's my turn anyway," offered one of the guards.

Throughout the day, members of the security team had been taking turns walking through the floors of the museum, checking for any potential hazards that might endanger its collections. Now that it was almost midnight, Joanne knew it was time for her to search the museum as well. If only she knew exactly where she was supposed to be when the new year arrived.

"May I go with you?" Joanne asked Russell.

"I would like to come too." Joshua jumped up, though he spoke softly.

Russell gave them both stern looks but did not refuse them.

The group of four walked quickly and without speaking. Outside, the lashing storm sounded as if it were curling itself, dragon-like, around the museum. The group tried to ignore it while walking through the second floor and then down to the first, where the security lights had gone out completely. The two security guards turned on their flashlights and waved their beams across the Grand Gallery whose centerpiece was the Great Canoe.

"Looks like there might be a broken pipe somewhere," said Russell, referring to water that had seeped in and formed puddles on the floor."

"Who knows, this beauty may once again serve the purpose for which she was created," noted the other guard, pointing his flashlight at the canoe.

They continued walking together toward the Hall of New York State where Joshua stopped in front of the diorama *An October Afternoon Near Stissing Mountain.* Joanne walked up beside him while the two security guards continued. The diorama was still and unhelpful. Noah's mother looked at Joshua, who stared at the world within.

"I think we need to keep up with them," she told him softly.

They caught up with the two guards and were walking through the Hall of Biodiversity, when up ahead they heard a thud that sounded as if something had fallen onto the floor. Joshua was the first to run toward the sound, though Joanne and the two guards quickly followed. When they arrived at the Theodore Roosevelt Memorial Hall, they all stopped and stared. There, standing in a puddle on the floor in front of the diorama of New Amsterdam, was an apparition. Joanne stared at the boy who, dressed in animal skins, looked like a refugee from a long-ago century. The boy turned to her. He held up a small twig to which a leaf and an acorn were attached and smiled.

# Part Five: The Return of Hope

# Chapter 26

The early spring was a wintery cold one. Unyielding patches of icy snow remained on the ground well into the season. When the weather did begin to warm, the melting snow left the earth covered in slushy mud puddles. Tiny brown buds, no larger than raindrops, began to appear on tree branches, and the blue-gray woods of winter became a hazy olive brown.

Soon, the tree buds opened, and the forests were laced with many shades of green and tinged with rusty reds from the flowering oak and maple trees. Tiny white flowers sprouted up from the mud, and everywhere the steadfast evergreens added contrast, anchoring the otherwise ethereal landscape. After a winter so brutal that all Tessa wanted to do was keep warm and sleep, the arrival of spring felt like the return of life itself.

The more beautiful the world became, the more work there was to be done. Throughout the river valley, families began building homes and preparing their lands for planting. Once a week, Elan was given a day off from his work at the settlement farm. While the farmer and his family spent the day in prayer and rest, Elan returned to help his own family. One day, as Elan began to clear the small piece of land that he intended for his apple orchard, Tessa gathered up her courage and asked him to help her search for spring seeds.

It was still early in the season, and there were not a lot of seeds to be had, but Elan agreed to help Tessa look for those they could find and for plants and trees whose seeds they could later claim. As they hiked to a nearby mountain, Tessa easily kept up with Elan over the wild and slippery terrain. Together, they climbed the steep trail that led to the mountain's summit. Once there, they sat side by side, Tessa wrapped in a woven shawl and Elan in a leather mantle.

The spring landscape was filled with the aromatic scents of flowering trees and plants. Everywhere, there was new life. At the base of the mountain, Tessa spotted ant-sized deer nibbling on tender green shoots. Overhead, two red-tailed hawks flew among the returning songbirds, who moved like tiny dust particles across a puffy, white cloud. As they sat beneath the spring sun, Tessa stole glances at the young man whose profile was backed by the cobalt blue sky.

Over the next few weeks, as the weather continued to grow warmer, spring seeds appeared everywhere. The new seeds were of many different shapes and sizes. They twirled to the ground and were blown about by maelstroms of spring wind. Some were embedded in the centers of tiny, papery kites, while others were surrounded by cottony white parachutes. Tessa chased after them and gathered up as many as she could.

On one of her expeditions into the woods, Tessa discovered an amber-colored, moss-like substance beneath a group of oak trees. Ignoring the fact that the stuff made her sneeze, she picked up a small clump and pulled it apart. The substance separated into little thread-like strands that bore tiny flowers. Later, Elan explained that they were the tiny male flowers of oak trees. Having finished pollinating the oak tree's female flowers, they fell to the ground in soft piles.

After learning how oak trees created their seed-bearing acorns, Tessa couldn't help but worry about Noah and the acorn he had brought back to their world. She would not find out if the Great Oak's offspring had germinated until she returned home with her seeds. If the acorn had germinated, then the seeds she had gathered would be allowed through the portal. If not, only she would be allowed through, and the seeds would remain behind.

Tessa was to leave Elan's world at the time of the summer solstice. She would return home on or by Independence Day. It had been less than a year since she entered the world of the past, but to her, it seemed like a lifetime ago. Now fifteen, she was no longer a sickly girl, but a strong and fully capable one who had learned to do many new things. She was a different person now and even though she had not recently seen herself, she knew that she looked different. Part of her wished she could return to her school and foster home just so she could show herself off to everyone.

In truth, Tessa was very anxious about her return home. When it was time for her to travel back, Taman and Ayanna brought her not to the mountains, but to an area by the ocean. It took them over two days in the horse-drawn cart to reach the pretty bay where another portal was thought to be situated. When they arrived, Tessa immediately ventured out alone to search for it. She did not know what she was looking for, as neither she nor Taman had any idea what form the portal would take.

As Tessa walked through the woods that bordered the bay, she heard the voice of a single pigeon cooing. Following the sound, she discovered a group of doves gathered on two leafy trees whose entwined branches formed an archway. Through these trees, Tessa saw a path, surrounded by gardens that led to a large house overlooking a turquoise sea. The scene did not look like one that belonged to Taman's world.

Quickly, Tessa returned to Ayanna and Taman, who helped her unload the three seed-filled jars from the back of the cart. Tessa carried each of the jars to the doves' trees where she pushed them through the archway. On the archway's other side, the entwined trees that had been full of the green leaves of summer now bore the pink flowers of early spring. Tessa, and the jars, had entered into a century that existed somewhere between her own and Taman's time.

While walking through the beautiful landscape, Tessa spotted what looked to be a disruption in the atmosphere. Further along the path something, seemingly invisible, blocked the view of the ocean and gardens behind it and reflected all that was before it. Cautiously, Tessa walked up to what was a clear and glassy rectangular shape.

Looking into the mirrored doorway, Tessa saw herself backed by the archway of flowering trees. Just past her reflection, she saw the shadowy forms of a small group of people. Before Tessa walked through the open portal, she looked carefully at her reflection. She looked nothing like the girl she had last seen in a mirror seven months before. Touching her hair, she smiled softly to herself. Ayanna had been right—her disease had not been allowed back in time.

Elan had told Tessa that Noah would probably be waiting for her in the museum. She only hoped he would recognize her. Holding her breath, she carefully pushed one and then the other seed-filled jars through the doorway to the future. She felt her heart sink as they each disappeared. Then, closing her eyes, she too stepped through.

Tessa arrived in a diorama that depicted a bird sanctuary once located at Theodore Roosevelt's home in Oyster Bay, New York. With relief, she saw her three jars sitting on the diorama's floor. They had made it into the future. Picking up the first jar she'd made, Tessa hugged it tightly to her chest. The sound of distant thunder brought her back to her surroundings. Looking out, she spotted Noah, his parents, and Joshua standing in the middle of the great hall.

"There she is!" Tessa heard Joshua yell.

"Those are just fireworks. We're celebrating the Fourth of July," Joshua called to her.

"Yes, I know. Has the acorn really sprouted?" Tessa asked the group that now gathered around the diorama.

"The acorn is now a lovely seedling," said Noah's mother, who reached out to help Tessa bring herself and the jars into the museum.

"We are so happy to have you back, Tessa. You look beautiful." Noah's mother hugged her.

"And it looks like you brought us something," said Noah's father, who also hugged her.

"These jars are filled with seeds. Now that the acorn is growing here, they will grow here as well," said Tessa.

"The little seedling is growing taller and stronger each day," said Noah's father. "We are going to be moving to the mountains in August and we are hoping to bring the seedling with us. Right now, it's in one of the greenhouses at the institute."

"I wish I could see it," said Tessa.

"I am so happy you are back, Tessa," said Joshua. "One day I might forgive you for nearly ruining my life."

"I am sorry, Joshua, I never thought I would get you in trouble."

"It's okay," said Joshua, who smiled sadly and then hugged her as well.

Tessa looked over at Noah. He had not greeted her. Instead, he remained where he was, his arms folded across his chest. For months, she had worried about him and longed to see and talk to him. She didn't understand his cold reaction.

"Tessa, I have spoken to your caseworker at the foster care agency about your becoming a part of our family. There is a lovely school in the mountain town where we will be living. Think about it, okay?" said Noah's mother.

"I don't think she's interested." Noah suddenly spoke.

"What's wrong, Noah?" his mother asked him.

"Why don't you tell them?" Noah addressed Tessa.

"You don't understand. I can breathe there," she called out to him.

"It's summer here. We would all breathe better there," Noah replied.

"What are you talking about?" Joshua looked at them both.

"My parents and sister are no longer here," Tessa cried.

"But we're also your family," Joshua said pleadingly.

"Tessa, do you have people waiting for you there?" asked Noah's mother.

Tessa remained quiet as tears came to her eyes.

"Why can't we all go back? It beats spending the summer in cooling shelters," asked Noah. "Dad, I know I tried to describe it to you. There are unbelievable trees everywhere, too many even. You can drink this amazing water from the streams and lakes that are everywhere and when you can't, you can drink beer. You can eat fresh fish, oysters, and real meat. Everyone wears fur there—and Mom, you will have to accept that. We could bring our whole family and Joshua's and Miguel's too. There is so much more space there than there is here. We could create our own village and live by ourselves in the mountains. It is true that the culture is a more primitive one. I mean in New Amsterdam, people get hung for ridiculous reasons. But there are some wonderful people there, and we can teach them so many new things."

"We need to stay here, Noah," his mother interrupted. "You need to stay here with us."

"Won't you miss books and your artwork? And what about school, Tessa? You love going to school," Joshua pointed out.

"I will miss school," Tessa replied trying not to cry.

"Do you really want to return by yourself to Elan's world? The new settlers will bring in all kinds of diseases for which they don't have cures," Noah pointed out. "Oh, and try to remember how colonists regarded girls who talked to their cats."

"Let's not do this." Joshua looked at Noah sadly. "I think Tessa has made up her mind."

"Noah, my illness is not allowed back in time. In the world of the past, I might get another illness, but at least I won't have this one anymore. If I stay here, I might not live to reach my twenties."

"I'm sorry!" Noah said, looking down at the floor.

"A lot of teachers and kids at school will miss you, Tessa," said Joshua softly.

"No, they won't, but thank you," said Tessa, wiping tears from her eyes.

"Tessa, if you ever change your mind and want to return to our time, we will be here for you," assured Joanne Bradbury.

"Thank you," Tessa replied, tearfully.

Then taking her leather purse off her shoulders, Tessa reached into it and took out two clay pendants that were strung with beads on leather cords.

"I made this eagle for you, Joshua. You are brave and see things from a higher point of view. One day you will soar high to a place of your own."

Tessa then turned to Noah. He remained standing in his spot, his arms still folded across his chest.

"I made this pendant for you. Taman told me that like the wolf, you don't give up and most importantly, you are a loyal friend. He also insisted that I give you this," Tessa then took the arrowhead she had found from her leather purse.

"Even though we have not known each other for very long, I feel that you are a brother to me. We will see each other again one day. You will see them all again," assured Tessa. She handed Noah's mother the pendant and arrowhead he would not accept from her.

Tessa then climbed back into the diorama. She did not wave goodbye but looked at everyone intently as if trying to memorize them. As she disappeared into its background, birds of all kinds filled the diorama of Oyster Bay. Like members of an army battalion, they stormed out into the museum. Flying in pairs, cardinals, finches, chickadees, sparrows, seagulls, robins, and crows circled the room, impatient, hungry, and aggressive like life itself.

# Chapter 27

In October, one year after he'd entered the diorama, Noah woke up in the middle of a hot night in his new but already cluttered bedroom. He'd been having a dream in which he was sitting on a bus parked across the street from the American Museum of Natural History. In the seat next to him, was a girl he assumed had been Tessa. He wasn't sure though, because the girl was looking out the window and turned away from him, and all he could see of her was her brown hair. Outside the window, wild white flurries of snow blew around the Hayden Planetarium whose glass dome seemed to sparkle within. Noah reached out to the girl, but before he got her attention, he woke up and the dream was lost.

Noah sat up in bed and brushed hair away from his hot and sweaty forehead. Since returning from the world of the past he'd insisted on wearing his hair longer, and it now fell over his eyes and landed just below his chin. Unable to fall back to sleep, he got up, tiptoed downstairs to the family room, and sat down at the oak table.

The new house had the same warm atmosphere as the apartment back at the institute. The quilt was still draped over its rack and the afghan over the couch, the paintings hung on the walls and new shelves were filled with his family's collection of old books. Located just a few blocks away from where his father's parents lived, the house now felt like home.

The house was quiet, as everyone else in it, even the cat, was sound asleep. Noah knew he should return to bed, but the dream had agitated him and he wanted to take a walk. Grabbing his backpack, he snuck out of the house and began to follow a sidewalk's trail of cracked rubber pavement. The sidewalk led Noah past an office park where newly planted walnut and syca-more trees grew, around and between several office and apart-ment buildings, to an institute-sized industrial park.

Walking into the park, Noah carefully avoided triggering the motion-sensitive security system as he made his way to the lake at its other end. He arrived at an area occupied by a man-ufacturer of cubes made from reclaimed Styrofoam. The white cubes that were used in building construction glistened beneath the park's lamps and reminded Noah of snow.

Sitting down in a shadowy space among the stacks of foam, Noah looked out at the lake. He reached into his backpack for his oxygen bottle and took a deep breath as a drone approached, humming overhead like a hornet. Behind the lake, the moun-tains continued to bear their silent witness to the world's unend-ing change. The entire region was now unrecognizable as the one where Taman's family had once made their home. Less than a year ago, Noah had seen with his own eyes the forests and networks of pristine lakes and streams that were once here. Now, most of the trees were gone, and the lake before him emanated an odor of sulfur and other sweeter-smelling chemicals.

Noah searched his backpack for the arrowhead Tessa had given him. He had allowed himself to accept this gift from her, although he still couldn't wear the wolf pendant she'd made him. When Noah's mother told him how calm and in control Joshua had been while being questioned by authorities, Noah thought that Tessa should have given the pendant to him. If anyone was a wolf, surely it was Joshua.

Noah now carried the arrowhead with him everywhere he went. Cut like a gemstone, its smooth, faceted surface felt cool to touch, and when Noah felt anxious, he pressed it against his palm and felt reassured. Noah had given everything he brought back from his journey to the museum: the pack he'd gotten from Taman and all the things Ro had given him, including the fur wrap and leather pouch. In return, he was given the origami whale that had hung from the hemlock tree.

Noah had not been to the museum since Tessa's return. For now, this was perhaps for the best. The portal would no longer open for him and he was struggling to accept that. His mother had been right, his place was here in the present where he had work to do. But Noah hoped to return to the museum soon. He planned to become a scientist just like his father. A scientist who would know from firsthand experience that not all phenomena can be understood logically.

After he had returned with the acorn, Noah, with the help of his parents and Joshua, concocted a story that explained both his and Tessa's disappearance. They told media outlets that

Noah had become lost due to an illness from which he had since recovered. They explained that Tessa, having been influenced by Noah's vanishing act, had staged her own to escape from an unhappy home life. Everyone was assured that she was now living with a new family in an undisclosed location which, ironically, was the truth. Only a few people, including those who were at the museum on the night Noah returned, knew what had really happened.

When Joshua was cleared of all suspicion, the institute offered to reinstate him. But Joshua was so hurt by their rejection that he refused to return to school there. Instead, at the suggestion of Noah's parents, Joshua's mother moved her own mother and two sons up north into the same apartment complex where Noah's maternal grandparents now lived. At their new school, where both Noah and Joshua were in the eighth grade, Joshua had become a sort of leader. Both boys made many new friends, one of whom was a girl named Zinny who reminded Noah of Tessa.

Though Zinny, with her hearty laugh and open smile, was far more outgoing than the sullen and often antisocial Tessa, there was something similar about them. In addition to looking alike, they both loved school, books, and art. But what struck Noah the most was the fact that Zinny wore a clay pendant similar to the ones Tessa had given him and Joshua.

"My mother gave it to me for my thirteenth birthday," Zinny explained, when Noah asked her about it. "She got it from her mother, who had gotten it from her mother, and so on. Who knows where the pendant came from originally? I come from a long line of women who love horses."

If Tessa had made a pendant for herself, Noah was sure it would have been that of her own spirit guide, the cat. Still, it was this conversation that gave Noah the idea to offer Tessa's cloth bag to Zinny. The bag had been left with Noah's mother to keep for Tessa, but now that Tessa belonged to the world of the past, she didn't need it.

"Her name begins with the letter Z," noted Joshua, when Noah told him of his intention.

"The letter T is designed like a tree. Why wouldn't Zinny like a bag with a tree on its front?" Noah had asked him.

"You are right. She'll probably love it," agreed Joshua. Of course she would!

After the Great Oak's acorn had been planted in one of the institute's greenhouses, Noah checked on it daily. When he finally spotted a tiny green shoot, barely visible in the dark potting soil, poking its nose up, he was filled with joy—and relief. The resurrected being brought hope into Noah's world, as it connected him to the past and everyone he had known and loved there.

The seedling grew quickly, and in August, when Noah's family moved upstate to the Catskill Mountains, they brought it with them. Noah and his dad planted it, along with other young trees and many of Tessa's seeds, in a state park. They decided to keep its identity and location a secret, and Noah knew that the Great Oak would have approved of this plan.

The Tree of Snow's descendent once again grew on the Earth. Soon after the seedling was planted in the park, it was reported that the treatment for the ailing trees that had previously failed, was now working. Scientists were noticing improvements in many hardwood trees. New leaf buds were forming on their branches, and their root systems were expanding. Noah's father had been skeptical about the acorn's supposed ability.

However, he knew that the treatment they were talking about had been completely ineffective.

Though Noah and his father were cautious about expecting too much from the young oak, they felt hopeful. The tree could not possibly solve all the environmental problems. But it would do its part, and maybe one day the Northeast's forests would be replenished and its animals given a chance at the lives they were meant to live. For now, Noah was content just knowing that his father was happy again.

Closing his eyes, Noah pictured Master James Giles and Elizabeth standing together on deck of the *Engel*, looking out to sea. He wondered if they had any descendants living in the world today. Noah would try to find them on a genealogy website. Then he realized something. In his dream, he'd assumed that the girl sitting next to him on the bus had been Tessa, but it just as easily could have been Zinny. At the moment, Noah did not want to think too much about what this might mean. He was tired and had to go home and try to get at least a couple of hours of sleep.

Before leaving the foam cubes behind, Noah took one more moment to remember everything he could about snow. He tried to recall the feeling of the blizzard's icy sting as he trekked through the woods and across the white field. But the heat of his present reality made this difficult. Maybe one day the tree really would bring back snow. But for now, only in dreams could the memory of its serene beauty be summoned.

As Noah walked home, the lights suddenly went out, and the world was submerged into darkness. Having no light-providing device, Noah began to panic before he remembered to look up at the night sky. There, from all over the universe, points of lights reached out to him. In his world, he had only seen this sight in the Hayden Planetarium. Finding the North Star, he thought about Taman and Eti. He envisioned Taman, looking solemn but pleased, and Eti, sitting in his round-topped house, smiling. Tessa had assured Noah that he would see them again. Like the stars overhead, maybe one day they too would just reappear.

As Noah looked up at the night sky, he filled with a feeling of hope and excitement. He wanted to throw his head back and send a prayer up to all those points of light, to call out to them and let them know he was here. But howling was not something Noah was about to do. Instead, with a tall, straight back and a solemn quiet dignity, he navigated his way back to the home of his family.

www.ingramcontent.com/pod-product-compliance
Lightning Source LLC
Chambersburg PA
CBHW020130120726
47903CB00007B/2189